DOGGIE STYLE

A tale of jealousy, sex and alcohol

by Fernando Nachón

Translated from the Spanish by Amy D. Prince

A translation of the novel *De a perrito* by Fernando Nachón.
De a perrito: first published by Federación Editorial Mexicana, 1986, republished by Fontamara, 1998.

Order this book online at www.trafford.com/07-2630
or email orders@trafford.com

Most Trafford titles are also available at major online book retailers.

Note for Librarians: A cataloguing record for this book is available from Library and Archives Canada at www.collectionscanada.ca/amicus/index-e.html

ISBN: 978-1-4251-5831-6

We at Trafford believe that it is the responsibility of us all, as both individuals and corporations, to make choices that are environmentally and socially sound. You, in turn, are supporting this responsible conduct each time you purchase a Trafford book, or make use of our publishing services. To find out how you are helping, please visit www.trafford.com/responsiblepublishing.html

Our mission is to efficiently provide the world's finest, most comprehensive book publishing service, enabling every author to experience success. To find out how to publish your book, your way, and have it available worldwide, visit us online at www.trafford.com/10510

www.trafford.com

North America & international
toll-free: 1 888 232 4444 (USA & Canada)
phone: 250 383 6864 • fax: 250 383 6804 • email: info@trafford.com

The United Kingdom & Europe
phone: +44 (0)1865 722 113 • local rate: 0845 230 9601
facsimile: +44 (0)1865 722 868 • email: info.uk@trafford.com

10 9 8 7 6 5 4 3

Contents

Preface

There are three basic genres in the Mexican literary tradition: the testimonial novel, the novel of magic realism, and the urban novel of the sixties' 'new wave'. Fernando Nachón belongs to none of these groups. Or rather, he appropriates aspects of each one, proceeding to turn them inside out, upside down, and back to front: any way but upright.

The testimonial novel has historically been used to present the author's political or religious awakening, told in autobiographical form and utilizing important decisions and conversations with key people in order to illustrate the character's personal development. Nachón's novel, *Doggie Style*, told in thinly veiled first person character, also tracks decisions and developments of his past as a means of presenting to the reader the events that have led him to his present condition. He, too, uses conversations with important people in his life to demonstrate his personal philosophy and reaction to the world around him. However, his life decisions, rather than being political or ethical, revolve around dilemmas such as which bar he will less likely be thrown out of, or whether the guilt and loneliness that comes with masturbation is worth the momentary pleasure. His revealing conversations, instead of being held with family members or intimate relations, are conducted with ex-girlfriends, analysts, and strange women in the mall. As for traces of magic realism, they appear in Nachón's work as paranoid fantasies and drug-induced visions. There are also pointed and sarcastic references to the 'great' Latin American writers; at one point Nachón, explaining why his books are often refused by bookstore buyers, says, "Anyway, they're all waiting for the last unpublished story by Borges."

Doggie Style belongs most closely to the Mexican writers of the sixties, writers such as José Agustín and José Emilio Pacheco, who broke with the mythical voice of Mexican fiction to create a new, urban voice. But rather than conform himself to a continuation of the themes and stylistic devices already known to Mexican readers, Nachón implodes the form, turning his work into at once an embrace and a rejection of city life, with Mexico City itself becoming a character, a live being that is criticized, berated, made fun of, and ultimately loved, as an inseparable part of the character himself.

Nachón—young, upper middle-class, and alienated, is a well-known type on the streets of Mexico City. Bored, horny, and always ready to escape through drugs or alcohol, he is painfully conscious of the absurdity of his situation, of his life. He is the first to criticize himself, and does so with an eagle eye and little sentimentality. The most endearing facet of his character, indeed, perhaps his one saving grace, is his recognition that he is part of a generation informed by "gringo appliances", "a social system based on North American television", and an obsession with neo-Freudian and neo-Marxist theoretical paradigms. "I'm an obnoxious rich kid," he says, moments before the reader reaches the same conclusion. He thereby invites the reader to relax, to enjoy his failures and his flings, because, in spite of every complaint and every whine, he obviously enjoys it all immensely.

Partly parody, partly straight, the most interesting aspect of the novel is that the reader cannot always distinguish between the two. "I must not be macho," Nachón says, "my friend Rogelio says it's just a petit-bourgeois disease." Yet two pages later he is at the mall, looking for a "little morsel", or being kicked out of a party for offering to fondle a strange woman's breasts. Vulgar, at times puerile, Nachón's desire to find meaning in his life nevertheless rings true, and his search for it leads him everywhere from transvestite bars to "pseudo-intellectual gatherings". "Are you trying to say you're not filthy rich, too?" someone asks him, after Nachón has accused him of only caring about his next trip to "Gringolandia". "I'm filthy rich when I fucking want to be," he retorts.

Both Nachón's style and language are highly reminiscent of Jay McInerney. Urban, disaffected, and using up-to-the-minute street slang, Nachón, like McInerney, paints a dismal, yet always humorous picture. "Ahh, how lovely it is to be a yuppie," he writes. "I can go slumming if I want to, and if not, I can hang out with the rich kids. But, oh destiny, they throw me out of both places." Nachón is quite aware of the power of language, both in creating a fictional construct and as a way to create an effect. Besides telling a story, *Doggie Style* is a book about language: language as a weapon, as a conceit, as a chicanery of satire, egotism, and manipulation. The level of irony that Nachón reaches leaves the reader stunned and exhausted as s/he attempts to make sense of the layers of language upon language, the smoke screens and mirrors he uses both to hide behind and to reveal himself. It is a world where not only names of products, but also ideas themselves are flung around carelessly, creating a literature of post-minimalism that assumes the universality of dogma as just more internationally recognized brand names.

Nachón, ever conscious of the potential audience he is speaking to, and ever despairing that in fact none exists, takes the reader through twenty-eight harrowing days and nights, roaming through Mexico City and spending one tortuous day in Jalapa, Veracruz. He apologizes for nothing, yet neither is he proud of his débacles. *Doggie Style*, in its combination of irreverence, irony, humor and pathos, reveals a world saturated with the very icons Nachón feels victimized by: language, sex, violence, hatred and banality. A world that, despite being set in Mexico, is all too familiar to anyone living in what we know as the modern world.

Amy D. Prince

One More Time

Suddenly everyone's telling me they're going to write the novel that will make them famous. Jesus Christ! All I had to do was publish a book and they all think I'm a writer. And now they want to write that book they've been thinking about for a long time. No matter how much I've explained to them the trick of throwing words onto paper they don't sit their butts down to do it.

Everything you do takes practice and I haven't practiced much. Just yesterday Mike told me so. "You ass! You still don't know how to write and you're ready to take Europe by storm."

The world is full of books, full of books that say the world is full of books. At the place that printed mine, all you have to do is scrape together a half million pesos and they'll publish your book. Make it incomprehensible, even 'Dadaist', give it to your friends, and when you die they'll say you were a writer.

It won't end up in the trash. I still don't know anyone who dares to throw a book directly into the garbage. It would be showing too much piety towards the writer. Anyway, you can always resell it; it'll usually end up on one of those bookshelves used for decoration, or as I've heard: "Give me a yard of Voltaire, preferably red."

Hardcover books, sitting in between two elephants or two Hercules with shields as the bookends, are never opened or given away. Nobody gives away a book. In Mexico City, the most polluted city in the world, and with a social system based on North American television, nobody gives away a book, much less a book they're never going to read. Those are the ones we care about the most; you never know when you might need them.

It's possible this book will end up stuck between two elephants or between a little statue of Horace and another one of Shakespeare, but if you've read this far, I swear you won't regret it; you'll find stories of sex and screwing, of dirty windows, of clean bureaucrats with dirty secretaries.

This is a dirty book. A disgusting book. Maybe this will be my immortal novel, the great novel I've been planning ever since I promised my friends I'd get the Nobel Prize.

But a novel isn't like a short story. A novel, so they say, must "create an atmosphere". The reader will sit down, ready to read a novel of at least a hundred pages. He'll have time to wander around in the words without having his view blocked by an image; he'll just be reading the book. The only voice this book has is the one you, reader, give it in your head. You can read it thinking in your own voice, you can do it in the voice of a friend, or in the voice of paranoia, or stoned, or maybe you just got up to take some poppers, or a snort, or a beer, or a tequila, or Valium, or speed, or you broke up with your girlfriend, or you're drinking pulque In *Los Dínamos.*

That's the problem with a novel; you have to take the reader by the hand so he doesn't get lost; you have to show him the way. Maybe you even have to be literary. Because if I'm not literary how the fuck am I going to write an immortal novel?

I'm sorry. I refuse to be 'literary'—I'd rather take you by the hand. Maybe you should just put this book down and find yourself some girl who's waiting for you in Sanborn's or somewhere like that; forget about her bodyguards—just go get her.

Now I see you've closed the book and you're going out to take a walk. Holy shit. So what the fuck am I doing here writing this? That's why I'm going to stop writing, get up, grab my jacket and walk two blocks to Avenida Insurgentes. On the way I stop to buy some Pingüinos cupcakes and a Chaparrita soda. While I'm drinking, I wonder if it will be a problem, and then I'm sure it will, to put 'Chaparrita' soda in one of my books; I could lose the Nobel Prize if they think my work is untranslatable. I turn away from a neon sign and close my eyes, swallowing the last of a pineapple Chaparrita. I think about how I only think about stupid things.

I just read the novel *Hunger*, by Knut Hamsun (Nobel Prize, 1920), and right now I'm under the influence of the way the main character speaks. I stretch out my hand to pay the saleswoman at the store and I feel like I'm on a street in Oslo. My mind is working like that character in Oslo. In my inane daydreaming, a man delivering Jarritos sodas arrives and bumps into me.

“Excuse me.”

I turned around to look at him; I wanted to tell him off, but seeing him busily lugging cases I felt guilty. “Poor guy,” I thought, “he was born poor and low class in one of the most racist countries on earth.” The woman gives me my change.

I leave, thinking of the novel I had just read; the character, for once, finds himself with a woman, a pre-imagined goddess he has named ‘Ylajali’ (maybe she’s the cousin of Comehereandoittome). I look for my semi-goddess between the hot asphalt and the hundreds of cars that wallpaper my corneas with a suffocating and disgusting smoke.

I escape to Sanborn’s, a cafe where they sell books, records, magazines, shit like that. Everyone looks like they’re in a bad mood. The floors are marble. They also sell VCRs, gold watches and other stuff. I feel trapped; there’s no sign of life in the people around me. I walk up to a plant that’s planted in sand; it’s plastic.

Fed up and dazed, I head back to the door. I see a woman pushing her baby in a stroller. She crosses the street; the baby’s cushiony little nostrils are plugged up with car exhaust, turning the pink skin into a viscous and black mucus that will stop up the condemned lungs like a dead placenta.

These thoughts cause me to suffer. “Yeah, I know, I should be like my friend Rogelio tells me, I shouldn’t be paranoid, I have to be positive.”

Fuckin’ Rogelio, what do I do now? While I’m thinking about what I should think about, my eyes light on some gluteus sheathed in a white fringed skirt, a delightful and delicate curve splashed with little white carnations that makes me feel happy and praise God for having given me eyes. My mind is thinking over and over, in a reverberation: “She has a perfect ass, she has a perfect ass.”

“Mamacita, I’ll kiss your ass if you want me to,” I thought. Ylajali, she was Ylajali, this was a delicious ass. I hadn’t recognized my goddess by the eyes, no! It was the ass, that pair of firm, meaty, tempting globes.

The woman made her way over to buy some chocolates; I followed behind her. She was wearing high heels so her bottom looked even bigger. I was stupefied; then I immediately felt ashamed. The security guards could see me staring right at her. I turned to look at them and no shit, they were also totally focused on her, until I swear I couldn't stand it anymore and I said to one of them, "What an ass she's got!"

"Oooh, mama!" he said.

The man's sincerity touched me; maybe he was someone intelligent who had to work in this shit job. The woman with the ass raised herself up on her toes as if looking for prices and her ass went right up with her. Then I saw it—the perfect asshole, round and perverse. Hidden between that line that separates the cheeks, that bifurcation, that line so many times crossed over, the battlefield of all great men.

Suddenly she turns around. I don't want to look at her face, I prefer to see the skirt spread across the front, simulating a V that encloses the delicious and furry pubis. About six feet away, I turn to look at her. It's an old woman with a blond dye job, sunken eyes, horrible double chin. A hideous woman, with heavy make-up from Liverpool Department Store, or Sears.

Never tell someone they're ugly (and I'm sure you never have). Beauty is the dividing line of all human beings, the division of worlds. Here in Mexico we have to be blond like gringos, but no, no, I shouldn't let myself think about those things. That's what my friend Rogelio says.

It's better just to go up to the woman, to go for it like Butragueño or Maradona after a goal. Besides, an ugly woman in candlelight or with incense is one of the most delicious perversions there are. If you add a bit of grass, you're on.

She leaves the cafe and walks to Insurgentes. She turns to the right. People going by in cars look at her; hers are a pair of buttocks worthy of being photographed. But when they pass by and see her face their eyes turn sad.

I catch up to her. "Excuse me, what's your name?" I say.

"Ursula," she says, coquettishly.

Her smile isn't as bad as the sunken eyes that make her look like a melting chicken, a chicken held together by Max Factor and Helena Rubenstein.

But, surprise! Suddenly I see her low-cut blouse, with a pair of huge and delicious breasts peeking out. Ooh, what lovely tits!

You can see the line of a shadow, and the bulk that shifts towards the front, ending in a nipple made erect by a cold wind that blows smog into our faces. Precious and chilled nipples, anxious for a mouth to suck them until they're hot and bothered.

While we were standing there on the sidewalk some assholes shout to her from a taxi: "I'll suck 'em for you, mamacita!" I didn't know what to say and I decided to laugh. Very somberly, like a dignified madman, I said to her, "It's just that, well it's true, you have very beautiful breasts."

I immediately regret saying it. In Mexico you can't say things like that; everyone's so full of hate and distrust. The smog has gone all the way to the hypothalamus. We're all becoming stupid and egotistical. That's why I quickly continue, "I could have said you had beautiful eyes, but the truth is your breasts are lovely." She smiled at what I said about her face. If she knew I'd followed her for her ass she would have told me to fuck off, but I got out of it by saying, "I like your eyes." I felt disgust and perversion in my comments.

I could tell right away she knew she was ugly; she didn't make any face to indicate it but the way she stood there, impassive, she was definitely thinking about her tight skirt, and the ass that discreetly hid a perfect crack.

Not knowing what to say, I automatically stuck my right hand in my pocket to look for cigarettes. I had some unfiltered Delicados. When I took them out I felt dizzy; the head of my penis was getting bigger, and the excitement left me speechless.

I knew I just about had her in my bed. I finally spoke. "Hey, are you doing anything right now?"

"Yes," she said, "I have to go meet a friend at Jeans, Jeans cafeteria, have you ever been there?"

Shit, that screws everything, now she'll go see her little friend and we'll have to sit and talk bullshit in a cafe. I'll say whatever they want, after I lay 'em; it is only without speaking that we can name ourselves. Damn broads.

"Come with me."

What woman says "come with me" in Mexico City two minutes after meeting you?

"Let's go," I said.

We barely spoke as we walked to the cafeteria. A dark-skinned woman with firm breasts and a divine rump approached us like a filly in search of a stud.

"Look," she said to me. "That's my friend Gabriela."

"Hi," I said. "What's going on, hey girls, let's go to my house. I'll make some coffee. It's no problem; don't go thinking I'm trying to pull a Mauricio Garcés. No, seriously, relax, it's just that I don't like being out on the street."

"Let's go," said the ugly one.

I let her go in front of me so I could watch the landscape of her flesh. We hadn't walked ten steps and I was already imagining doing it doggie style.

"And what do you do?" one of them asked me.

"I'm a psychoanalyst."

"How many years did you study?"

"Well, only for a little while; they threw me out for drinking. But I don't drink anymore. Don't think badly of me."

"Did you used to drink a lot?"

"Yeah."

"And how did you stop?"

"I'm in Alcoholics Anonymous."

"You don't have any alcohol in your house?"

"A bottle of gin, but just for other people who might want a drink."

The horsey one said, "I'm in AA, too." We all felt embarrassed. In those days being in Alcoholics Anonymous was uncool, like being of out the intelligentsia and everything that's normal.

We got to the apartment. The first thing I did was put on some rock music. Ursula took out a huge joint, lit it and passed it to me; I breathed in the wet and sacred liquid and felt new skins growing under my own. I thanked God that I was there among the marijuana smoke and so much flesh. I knew that in order to pass to the sexual plane I had to bring out the liquor; according to a psychology class I took, alcohol squashes the superego.

"Do you want a drink?" I asked Ursula. "Okay," she said.

As I walked over to the refrigerator I started to feel nervous, they might steal a couple of cassettes when I wasn't looking. I was worried and tense; that's probably the reason they came. Fuckin' broads. But no, Rogelio says I shouldn't be paranoid, that those are petit-bourgeois worries; that's what Rogelio says.

I took two still-greasy glasses out of the sink. There weren't any clean ones.

I went out to tell them it was going to be a while. Gabriela got up and met me at the kitchen door, lifting herself up like a sensual whale that rises up out of the sea. She pressed against my stomach with her two breasts. "Can I help you?" she asked.

"Okay," I said. I felt inhibited, and thought about drinking a gin and tonic. But no. Only for today, not today, today I am not going to drink, no! Remind yourself thirty seconds before you drink the first one what happened the last time.

Gabriela pours herself a gin over ice; it steams and makes a cloud in the shape of lips. The ice crackles and twirls as it melts. Then she adds some grapefruit juice and the ice magically begins to float. Gabriela closes her hand around the glass as if it were an erect penis; she brings it to her mouth and drinks it down while I watch her, puzzled: "What? Aren't you in Alcoholics Anonymous?"

"No," she says, "I was kidding. Aren't you going to have a drink?"

"Um, no, I'm not." Just for today, just for today; instead I'm going to fuck myself up on pot so I can pretend I'm drunk. "Hey, by the way, I discovered a great recipe: Valium and pot. It's fantastic; you take a pill, then you take a huge toke and you go into a sleep that's like a delicious death. You fall into a beautiful stupor, like you're really going to die, but it's so cool, you go flying around your room, above all the musicians and writers. You rupture the sky, you become at one with yourself."

She looks at me with her dark innocent eyes.

"You really like pot that much?" she asks.

"Yeah," I told her, "I love it."

"How many joints do you smoke a day?"

"Two or three."

"Ooh," she said, closing her mouth in a timid fear.

Soon we were sitting on the carpet. Gabriela grabbed the joint and sucked it in with vigor. Holding the smoke in, she asked me:

"So what do you think of the world situation?"

"It's fucked up," I say, also holding in the smoke. I can feel myself in a process of immersion. I keep it in as long as I can, until my bronchial tree feels the seeds of THC, the substance that makes us forget how Reagan wants to destroy the world. And if we're still worried, well we drink some gin, and that's it. Or take a Percodan, or do some poppers. And then, just to say something, I say to Ursula, who's looking at a painting:

"Hey, you know I once had this psycholinguistics professor who thought it was really boring to talk to people who were stoned. I guess it's like when someone talks about their dream in a novel, as interesting as it is, you know it's a trick. Of course, it depends on who's doing the talking, right? Yolanda Vargas Dulché isn't the same as Marcel Proust." While I was talking, Ursula started to lift up her shirt; you could see the skin below her tits, a bit irritated by the underwire of an ancient bra that pushed her boobs up in a phenomenal way.

Then she took off her shirt. Gabriela turned up the music and we started to dance like crazy. I saw the end of a joint in an ashtray, recognizing it as if it were a torch in the darkness. I lit it desperately, burning my moustache, and sucked in on it; when it started to burn my fingers I threw it down, but by then I had attained the essence of the divine mothers, and a good bit of smoke was now crying blues and rock in my lungs. I held in the smoke as long as I could; a thousand warriors were taking position on the horizon of my thought, but they were in peace. I had not yet consumed any alcohol, that terrible monster Ballbreaker who destroys men, girlfriends, and entire nights. I felt like having a gin. What the hell, Malcolm Lowry died drunk. He and a shitload of other great men. To forget about drinking, I made another gin for Gabriela. She saw that her friend had taken off almost all her clothes, and she didn't stay far behind. She pulled off her pants, and two dark thighs like columns of obsidian deep in the ocean glowed red from the candle that Ursula had lit.

She had on some luscious underwear. They were made of linen and had little red hearts printed on them. They were held up by strings that tied at the sides. "Gorgeous!" I thought. "If only my friends could see me!"

I hadn't seen underwear like this for years. This type of underwear is very useful when you're already in bed; there's no need to shift around, lifting up the girl's hips and motioning her to take off her underwear, for which she would have to flex her legs, and she still didn't have a lot of confidence in you, and you had to stop caressing her clitoris in time with the sax music—and the erotic thread could be lost. That's why this underwear gives us permission to play with the imagination.

It's strange, the psychoanalysts say that fetishes—garters, stockings, shoes—are just one more thing in a woman that signifies a penis. Such rational thoughts made my dick go limp, but I got it back up with a little squeeze, and with the fondling that Ursula was giving my balls. Oooh, my balls! Sacred eggs, holy sac, bag of life, expandable fabric, close and yet distant. Oh, how delicious! Gabriela begins to lick the head of my penis; it looks purple, and starts to drip a shiny lubricating liquid that shines and reflects the light of the lamp on the night table. "Wherever you look you'll find what you're searching for," Lacan said.

It's gotten dark. Or maybe it's the curtains, or the pot, or Gabriela's breast that's covering my mouth, a mouth that I'm using to suck her nipple like a man in agony, like a pariah wandering stupidly in the desert. Every now and then Ursula passes me a joint. As I hold in the smoke, I feel her mouth surrounding the fat and erect head of my dick like a moist wave of heat.

"This is the best moment of my life," I think. "I hate work, and decency. Long live pleasure, screwing, and rock and roll, fuck all the goddamn shit-filled institutions, beginning with the family." Ursula sucks me harder. Mmmm. I desperately look for some poppers but they're not on the night table. I don't see them anywhere. "What are you looking for?" Gabriela asks.

"My poppers," I answer. "It's a beautiful drug, you just breathe it in and you feel like you're speeding off in a plane; the whole thing lasts thirty seconds."

I go to turn the tape over and use the chance to take a piss; fucking with a full bladder is a bit uncomfortable. I look around for the poppers. Standing in front of the toilet, I feel strangely dizzy from getting up so quickly. Then it passes but now, for God's sake, I have to wait until my cock goes down a little so the urine can come out; I try to think of something else besides sex.

Yeah, I'll think about Ylajali, the character in the novel I finished yesterday. Neither of these two tramps was Ylajali. Ylajali, maybe she had already appeared and disappeared forever from my life. Where was she? Where would that Aleph in the shape of woman be found who would allow me to see all the disasters of the world, and all the pleasures? Where? "Holy shit," I thought, "I'll spend forty more years looking for her."

Then my dick came down a little and I began to piss. It came out in little spurts; I wasn't limp enough to get a thick flow going. I thought the girls must be getting impatient. I leaned out to make sure they weren't getting dressed, then went back into the room. They were still there—fooling around with each other. They were doing a sixty-nine. Gabriela stuck her tongue in the ass of Ursula, who was panting and sticking her tongue up Gabriela's. They looked like a number eight lying down, like a Möbius strip, like the sea, like infinity. I started to get it up again, and with an empty bladder, I went in for the attack.

I reached the edge of the bed and pulled Ursula into a doggie style. I entered her, breathing hard. "Good God," I thought, "remember that ass we saw on Avenida Insurgentes? Well now it's mine." I began to claw her buttocks with passion. "Move it, sister, move it!" her friend shouted at her.

I felt like I was navigating the Atlantic; I was on the prow of a big ship, I was the captain and was conquering virgin lands (and of course virgins). I pulled her hair like they were horse's reins, pulled it so she would throw her head back and make her ass go up even higher. Then Gabriela came over with a chopstick she had found in a drawer. She made me pull out of Ursula so I wouldn't be in the way and she shoved the chopstick up Ursula's ass, an ass which wiggled like it was sending us kisses. She moaned and she wiggled up to her spine; on the bed, waiting for me to give it to her doggie style, she looked like an immortal statue.

Gabriela wanted Ursula to turn herself on with the chopstick and open her legs as wide as possible so I could go in with my trunk.

Ursula turns over, opens her legs and puts them on my shoulders. I suddenly feel guilty for what I'm doing; I break out in a cold sweat, combined with a high state of excitement. I can't contain myself any longer; I come as soon as I enter Gabriela. They immediately realize what's happened. Half angry, they pretend they don't notice, and begin to fool around with each other again. Sad, and forever branded by my culture, I go into the living room.

Ooooooooh Shit

It's morning, or rather, afternoon. The women have gone. Distant, towering, disproportionately and even genetically, they have left me.

I'm alone; I remember just before falling asleep that the last of the women—my mother?—was giving me baby bottles of gin and brandy. I drank them all as if they were life-giving plants, plastic baby bottles, terrible plastic pariahs that carve out the mouth of a drunk.

I didn't know it when I drank the first one; I realized it after the third or the fourth, or when I listened to the tape player with the same music. Every cassette was the same music.

I remember daydreams of music repeating itself. I remember calling an ex-girlfriend, arguing with her about her lips being so far away, her lips, accommodating and almost perfect, her lips, melted by my old kisses. I remember I was lying through my teeth. Did I lie through my teeth? Did I even call her? I didn't remember.

The stupid genius of alcohol had allowed me to lie. I was a liar, full of pulsating eroticizations of the skin that flake off in frustration, to be replaced by that of a nice, polite guy.

Drinking is a beautiful thing! Drinking is a terrible thing! The phone rings; it's José Luis, a Lacanian friend of mine. Lacanian? Well, he's into Jacques Lacan, the Freud revisionist. Lacan, someone actually important in all the wave of idiots like me who clog up the streets.

José Luis was bummed because David Cooper had died; he said he was saddened by the death of a great intellectual.

A great intellectual who said "what needed to be said", who talked and talked, about the anal contractions of the British Prime Minister when she reads her speeches, for example. He talked about *The Death of the Family*, and *The Language of Madness*, and José Luis neither killed anyone in his family nor knew anything about madness; I could tell by the way he talked. "I'm be over in an hour. Maybe I'll come over, maybe not. If I do it'll be just to borrow *The Language of Madness*," he said.

"Are you coming over or not?" I asked him, half asleep and half drunk.

"I don't know."

"Why don't you know?"

"I just don't know, I have to go give a talk at a women's seminar; some girls you know are going to be there."

I knew just which ones they were! They had thrown me out of one of those seminars because I went there drunk and started cozying up to them. Now one of them, Susana, was married; she had found herself a little dog that wags its tail and follows her around on errands. Like all women, she had found a jerk who would support her.

She said she loved him, but how could she? How could a woman really feel love if she could refuse a happy alcohol-soaked poet like me? We hadn't even gone out together. A good thing, too. Her refusal to open her legs for me to while away the darkness had destroyed my liver and my spirit.

Oooh Jesus, what a drunken night; what a pain it is to carry around a hangover. A hangover is like Christ, who treats all of us equally, as if we were all his children and all his favorites. That's why God had sent me gin and brandy; he knew 1986 was a fucked-up year. It was part of the eighties: neon lights, punks who try to be bad and end up good; women who try to be good and end up bad.

Ah, the eighties! Time of great literature, time of fucking hell on earth! The situation was so bad here in the concrete jungle that everyone called it just that. Yesterday was the inauguration of the peace conference between Mexico, Argentina, Tanzania, Sweden, India and Greece. It was a gathering of 'The Six'. Six presidents had met in Ixtapa to talk about the same bullshit they've talked about for centuries, so many meaningless centuries.

Hung-over and feeling useless, I got up to pour myself some gin. A simple gin on the rocks. Just one, just one drink, one gin, one imbecilic, transparent and ethylized way to be able to live with myself.

I remember that José Luis, the Lacanian, hung up after telling me I was on the road to ruin. He tried to make me feel better by telling me I was like Christ, carrying all the sins of humanity on my back. I told him he was an egotist, just like everyone else, that David Cooper had written so they'd actually put his words into practice, not so it'd be fashionable to read him after he died.

Borges had just died and all the newspapers were filled with him. Quoting Borges would cause people to stare down at the ground, filled with sorrow. My father died on July 1. I had felt sad, and ridiculous, when I heard that Borges had gotten married while my father was lying in bed in agonizing pain. Then Borges died and my father was still in pain, in pain and cracking jokes. Jokes he made up to scare away the vultures while we gave him glasses of water. Jokes that made my throat open up as if they wanted to turn me into a poet then and there—a grand poetic destiny—while my father stained the sheets with death and with a nostalgia that sooner or later would catch up with me.

Even José Luis had said to me, like a good Lacanian, that I was left emptied and lost by the death of my father. "You're on your own now," he said.

Ocho y Medio

Yesterday, after my premature ejaculation and my first gin, I went out for a drink at El Colegio. There were some construction workers there who calmed me down me with their precocious and vacuous dialogue. The conversation of unintelligible drunks is just like the ones between a close and hateful family.

One of the workers asked me what I did. I said I wrote.

"What do you write?"

"I'm doing a novel."

"What's it going to be called?"

"*Doggie Style*," I told him. "It's sort of in the style of *Hopscotch*; all the characters I write about end up doing it doggie style. Then at the end I do it too, and death comes to me through the ass."

"Sounds interesting," he said, raising a rum and coke or a vodka tonic or some wine. It didn't matter; the thing was to keep drinking. Meanwhile, six chief officers kneel down before Ronald Reagan asking for clemency from being destroyed by nuclear arms.

The truth is it's okay to kneel down to the United States; everyone's done it one way or another. It's okay because it's the best way to conceal our stupidity and our cowardice.

That premature ejaculation yesterday was really strange. I get up to look for some more gin. The longing for the free world awaits me. I know of no pleasure greater than self-destruction through alcohol. I pour myself a gin. I think of you and your immortal novel. I believe and believe again that David Cooper's dead.

I remember the hangover that was crawling all over me then. But now, everything is beautiful, with my glass of gin at one side, songs strung together that create new songs, and a classy rich-kid telephone—just like the one Rogelio has next to his bed.

Too bad the cord of this goddamn telephone is really the umbilical cord of a dead placenta. On the other end of the line is everyone else in the world; and of them all, not one man who will help me start the revolution, and too many women who want to castrate me. My God, there's no saint I can pray to who'll get me out of this one.

1986. I clearly remember Mike telling me:

"Nooo, man, you gotta write a novel that synthesizes the decadence of the eighties. We'll sell ten thousand copies!"

"Something like *One Hundred Years of Solitude*?" I asked him, hoping for something more helpful on his part.

"Don't be stupid," he said, looking absently at the wall.

Suddenly the telephone rings. It's Rogelio. He's calling me to ask if I'm going to the disco, to Ocho y Medio.

He knows I can't go; the owner, François—you pronounce it fransuaaa—won't let me in. The thing is, Ocho y Medio is a gay disco, for queers, I mean. One time, bombed as usual, I said to François (fransuaaa; try to get used to it):

"Hey, this is a queer bar. And it's called Ocho y Medio because it symbolizes a man with half an erection, and anyway—hic—I think you're really a great guy, I just don't like it when you go with Jean Claude (you pronounce it Zhonclá) into the kitchen and speak French and you both ignore me, besides it makes me want to grab Jaime by the tits when he dresses up like Maria Victoria."

"Watch it, watch it, you just watch out!"

While I was talking to him I was hanging onto his arm, begging for a drink. I think my drunken and assholeish attitude frightened him.

Ocho y Medio was the sweetest road to ruin; New York decor, alcohol-filled nights, rivers of rum, and punks, who, like I said before, tried to be bad and ended up being good. Claudio was there, looking beautiful as he doused his ulcer with liquor, and Claudia too, with the face of someone who has to drag her family around with her everywhere. I also saw the short guy who worked as a garbage collector. "So? Drunk again?" I said to him.

"What's it to you?" he answered. "And what about you, you still got that beer belly?" Fuckin' jerk.

In Ocho y Medio all the vices and the anxieties of the eighties were mixed up together. You only had to stay there a hundred years and you would find out where the gaps in this decadent system came from; really it was Ocho y Medio's own decadence that made it so luxurious; it was the style in which we went outside two by two to vomit, so we could go back in and start drinking again.

It was Lucía, a beautiful transvestite, happy because they had just operated on her ribs and now her waist was the size of an ant's. Obsidiana, another drag queen who smelled of whiskey, talked to me about the pros and cons of castration.

"No, dear, the thing is, the majority of boys who have the operation later start to crave women, can you imagine? They turn into lesbians. Others get into pills and then kill themselves. What should I do?" she said.

"Just stay like you are and have fun."

"But the clientele is going down, you don't see too many anymore who realize what all the bulk is. There are some who, no matter how much you make something up about having your period and that it's just Kotex, they want to see it, and they don't take any shit. Think of what us men have to go through. Women, I mean."

"Hey, Obsidiana, so how do you do it then? Hic."

"Well, I get them when they're drunk and that way they don't notice, at least not until they tip me."

"How much do you charge?"

"For a Frenchie?"

"What's a Frenchie?"

"Oh come on, a Frenchie's a blowjob. And for a blowjob I charge two thousand pesos."

"Shit, that's nothing."

"That's right, my dear. And it's disgusting work, too; the other day they took me to this thirteen-year old Jewish kid's house, they said they just wanted him to have some fun; he peed in my mouth."

Obsidiana was cracking up; I was happy, too, with power in my glass, as if ten thousand brave warriors were behind me.

"Gimme a double rum and coke!" I shouted.

They gave it to me. 'Maldita vecindad y los hijos del quinto patio' would get up on stage to play, or sometimes 'El Tri' or 'Eku Kale'. And they would parade across the stage while we, like caged schizophrenics, like gremlins, like people condemned by the hydrogen bomb, like happy rats, jumped and danced. The waiters would grab the really rowdy ones and roll them down the stairs to the street. That was the best part; it reminded me of Bukowski, who said: "Writing is like tumbling down a flight of stairs."

When they pick you up like that, and you're totally smashed, held up by a couple of bastards, and you don't give a fuck about anything, all you do is watch the world spin and time go by. I remember a skinny guy who claimed he was a black belt kicked me in the face. Another bastard ran me down like a bus, then kicked the shit out of me while I curled up on the stool so he wouldn't reach any organs.

I got no respect at Ocho y Medio. I realized this between rounds with the waiters, as I recalled the beginning of Proust's *Remembrance of Things Past*: "For a long time I used to go to bed early. Sometimes, when I had put out my candle, my eyes would close so quickly that I had not even time to say 'I'm going to sleep'. And half an hour later the thought that it was time to go to sleep would awaken me; I would try to put away the book which, I imagined, was still in my hands, and to blow out the light." That's what I thought about while they were beating me up. About the fact that I remembered Proust, the fact that in my soul I reassembled the words one by one, that I was reliving the tranquility of going to sleep and of dying, drunk, while they were hitting me. Later Mike told me:

"What!? If you went there to start something, you might have well have just said, 'Go ahead, hit me, it doesn't hurt at all!'"

But I didn't go there to start anything. No, the thing is these guys were François' secret police; they had taken on the role of police and that was it. They punched me in the stomach and as they did it I heard the words of Marcel Proust again: "For a long time I used to go to bed early." I remember the words and the sound bringing me a tranquility and a calm that made me sleep and die at the same time.

Drunk, curled up, protecting myself from the blows.

What did they expect me to say? Be nice, you assholes? Bureaucrats even are worse than you are? You would still hit me in this condition?

"You would still hit me in this condition?"

The telephone rings. It's Mike, telling me I can go to Ocho y Medio after all. After I hang up I take another slug of gin, then I remember I'm in Alcoholics Anonymous; after I remember that I take another big swig. It's possible that I'm dying in the long run. I don't know which is worse, the torture of alcohol or deciding whether to drink or not.

Drinking makes me remember Proust, with his delicious, clear language, as if my soul were sure to die in one long, tranquil dream. I think about my mother, how I used to harass her when I was young, asking for glasses of sugar water. She would bring them to me and put them on the night table, almost in an attitude of prayer. She never imagined that I would be staring at that same night table years later with a killer hangover, in a stupid and cursed void. My mother always brought me the sugar water. A glass that looked right at me, with love and desire frothing up out of it.

As I got ready to leave for Ocho y Medio, I was feeling tense; maybe the bouncers at the door would go after me again. Besides, I had to get into the car: "Alcohol plus an automobile equals homicide." In this drunken delirium I could weave off the road and kill an entire family. But still I pick up the keys, find the one for the motor, and grab a small bottle of Oso Negro vodka.

I stagger to the elevator; in my stupor I remember how different we alcoholics are from sober people. When I'm sober, I can't understand drunks either. But right now it's another story. Yes, I make it to the car; I turn on the ignition and immediately take another swig of Oso Negro. "How intense, I'm an alcoholic; I'm a victim of commercialism and the crappiness of my own existence," I think.

I turn on the radio. By a stroke of luck Dire Straits is on. I step on the gas. I'm king of the road. I pass everyone without stopping. Before I know it I'm at Ocho y Medio. At first they don't want to let me in. "Look at me!" I say to François. "Look me in the eyes and you will be forgiven!"

François laughs coquettishly, half drunk and in a good mood; he averts his eyes until I grab him by the cheeks and say in a Freudian voice that Freud himself couldn't hypnotize his patients because he couldn't look people in the eyes. Finally he looks straight at me, relaxes, and lets me into the bar.

Aaarrgghh

The minute I enter I know I'm in Ocho y Medio. How can I explain it? Ocho y Medio is sort of like the subway, but with more neon lights and more colors. Transvestites, sculptors, painters, intellectuals who wanted to be cultured and ended up alcoholics.

As soon as I go in I see Rogelio. I go straight for his rum and coke and take a big slug. People look at me strangely. They don't understand why I'm drunk if I'm supposedly in AA. I quit AA because sobriety bored me stiff; I stopped going to the meetings because I couldn't stand listening to advice from people who hadn't had a drink for two years, as if that made them cultured sophisticates. I stopped going to AA because my 'sponsor' (that's what they call the ones who help us not to get drunk) told me he had masturbated thinking of my girlfriend. I told him to go fuck himself.

The important thing is I was back there once again, and Ileana, a transvestite, was rubbing my ass in greeting. Rogelio's looking at a girl; they're talking about rock and shit.

Since the minute I got there, a bunch of queens have been buying me drinks and asking me why I'm straight. They try to convince me that anal sex is better, because you feel it all the way up to the prostate; they say it tickles and makes for an abnormally tremendous ejaculation. Up till now no one has been in there. Could I be out of fashion?

I don't know if I was just too drunk in Ocho y Medio and that's why everyone else looked so drunk to me, or if it's because they really were. They were all pretty nice to me, because I talked with my heart on my sleeve. Later, when we were hung-over, Rogelio bawled me out because I gave vulgar nicknames to all the girls: Black Pussy, Wanda the Worm, Patty Titty. Rogelio freaks out easily. What the bastard doesn't remember is that when he went to guzzle beer with his buddies he started slow dancing with Marcos, the painter, and trying to sing like Pedro Infante.

I remember only alcohol and alcohol. There was a girl who was crying because she couldn't find her purse and I and a bunch of other assholes tried to convince her that she had come there just to make love to us.

I told her she should do it at least to help me stop drinking. At that moment, it was only a girl who could help me to stop. I also remember saying to a bunch of them: “Don’t you know that skin has many similarities with alcohol?” I would bullshit them to see if that way one of them would go with me and we could forget about the destruction of the liver. In Ocho y Medio we were all cirrhosising like crazy. Of course, there were one or two who went just to dance, but the truth is the entire world of intellectual decadence was there in that room. If Gramsci had only seen us! Almost all the drunks who were there were supposed members of the left. Even Rogelio, who now believes more in atomic war than in class struggle. Or Mike, who now wants to be a millionaire. Chill out, Scrooge Mike Duck. Give me a break.

They just wouldn’t leave me alone! They threw me out of Ocho y Medio again and I decided to go to a party at Ibero University, in the classy Pedregal section of San Angel. It was a graduation party for political science students. They didn’t like it that I swore in front of the girls. “Oh, like you’ve never heard someone swear before!” I shouted at them. And bam!—someone punched me right in the head. Since I had been drinking for three days straight. I was sort of out of it. I got back up and then someone shoved me. Back down again. I didn’t have time to protect myself and I felt two kicks in my face like gunshots in succession. I liked seeing my blood on the ground. I thought when the little preppies saw my blood they’d get scared, but it just made them want more. They grabbed me by the hair and started in on my stomach. At that point I managed to curl up so they couldn’t get at me. They went back inside. I stood up again. “Fuckin’ yuppies!” I shouted after them. “You all just want to be gringos! You only study political science so you can exploit the workers! Your whole world is American football and going to MacDonald’s for hamburgers.” Then some short guy walked over to me. “Calm down, man,” he said.

“What?” I said to him. “Oh, you must be the leader of the pack. Don’t you know the head of the institution is the most yellow of ’em all? Don’t you all realize what Bertolt Brecht said?” (I quoted Brecht to them to see if I could save myself from another blow, maybe they’d think I was educated.) “Yeah, Brecht said we must tell the truth! He said we live in a social system based on torture!” Two guys came out and punched me in the eye, laughing like a pair of cowboys.

"Sure!" I shouted at them. "All you talk about is your last trip to Gringolandia! You're all fuckin' losers!"

"So what?" the short guy with the Pierre Cardin shirt said. "You trying to say you're not filthy rich, too?"

"I'm filthy rich when I fucking feel like it! You're just Rogelio's fucking whore!"

I knew it was useless: the revolution was over; people were into different things now. Before I left I squeezed my nose to get it to bleed more. My hand was smeared with blood and I wiped it on a gringo van that was parked at the door.

I turned around. A big line of Corsairs, Magnums, Grand Marquis, Atlantics and other cars were parked at the curb.

I went to my house in Pedregal. My mother was out of town. I knew my analyst would interpret my going as a tug on my neurotic umbilical cord. Or maybe it's not neurotic. Even Freud said, "The mother's favorite son is the one who wins." Some of his disciples contradicted him. Who knows? The thing is I called my mom long distance, to tell her I was pissed off because no one was letting me start the revolution. Not the ones on the right, not the ones on the left.

I imagined my mother must feel like Christ's own. I, delirious and drunk, told her that yes, I was like Christ and I would kill myself when I turned thirty-three.

That was my mother! She for one supported me. She suffers when I get bombed. I remember when I tried to stop drinking I read her the alcoholic's manifesto.

And all for nothing. Here I was calling her, dead drunk.

She knew that you can't tell the truth, not in Mexico or anywhere else in the world, that whoever does is killed. That's also why I drank. Because of that. Because everything and because nothing.

I'm hung-over. I go in and out of it. I know if I don't drink I'll get delirium tremens. One time I decided to kill myself; I believed that at any minute an imperial command would invade my mind and I would kill myself.

Holy God! I hope I don't get delirium tremens. Since I've spent so many hours, almost entire days blacked out while I was drunk, I'm just waiting for someone to come tell me about some jackass thing I've done.

I call Mike, he's really pissed because I bothered his girlfriend the last time I was drunk. I say, "I don't remember, I was drunk."

"It's one thing to be drunk and it's another being an asshole to women," he says.

That means goodbye Ocho y Medio; they'll never let me in again. Oh well. Sniff.

"Hey," I say to him, "I'm still hung-over, I feel like I'm turning into a crab. The delirium tremens could come any minute and I'll go crazy from lack of alcohol. And how're you?"

"Just hanging out; I don't know if I should grow old or kill myself. Everything's so boring. There's no way to do anything."

"Okay," I say. "I just called to tell you I'm hung-over. If I don't turn into a crab I'll call you later."

"Cool."

We hang up.

Shadows

And what if you don't find the right words? Thinking is easy. But writing is another thing; suddenly nothing comes out and you sit there massaging your balls, waiting for Ylajali, hungry for a woman. Suicidally sick for it.

Coming out of a hangover, closed up in a cave of sweaty sheets, frightened, terrified, sweating, hearing my name called by a voice invoked by the alcohol as it reached my most delicate meninges. My entire nervous system was shot. But then I started to come back to life a little.

Son of a fucking bitch! When people go to the movies to see Pink Floyd, *The Wall*, or some other bastard suffer up on the screen, they don't bother to think that their neighbor is lying in bed, clutching the sides of the mattress. With a hard dick. Because yes, hangovers make you want to fuck. I remember I masturbated five times in the shower. At times I thought I would tear my dick off from the anxiety of it.

My urethra is damaged, it needs a girl to save it, it needs a kind father-in-law who won't torture it. My urethra suffers from solitude. The psychoanalysts still don't agree if there exists a urethral stage, where children play to see who can pee further.

My urethra would gallop around inside me all night. It doesn't only piss urine, but also alcohol and anxiety-scented semen. Every hangover is the same and every hangover is different. A hangover is like coming back to life and then seeing dead children on the news. Everything is horrible; even the most orthodox Marxist believes in God during a hangover. And what about those horrible hangovers where you can't stop thinking about death: of Cooper, Jean Genet, Borges, Simone de Beauvoir, Renato Leduc, the 'Indio' Fernández, the suicides in the tabloids, and the man sentenced to the electric chair for raping five girls.

Everyone dies, there's no one to talk to, the smoke from the cars rises up over Mexico City, Distrito Federal, and I still don't have a main character. I'm sorry Mike! This book isn't going to be the *A Hundred Years of Solitude* of the eighties. There's no Aureliano Buendías, or anyone else, here among the city rats, only hunger, and my urethra, spent and petrified by anonymity. Every minute a hundred and sixty children are born. Every day a thousand new books are published. Jesus fucking Christ! From the minute we're born, all we want to do is write. Speaking of that, I have to go register a bunch of stories and poems at the Society of Authors and Musicians. Luckily, my hangover and the delirium tremens have passed. But now comes another bad trip: reality. Argh!

Reality

Reality is a Jim Morrison record spinning without end, starting and ending and the needle going back in place and a dead man lying next to it after blowing off his head with his father-in-law's revolver. God sends me a sparkling white, loving joint. It's almost a whole one. I reach over to light it, but wouldn't it be better to save it for the traffic? To go out into the jungle of shit and cars and have this toke with me. What a relief. It's true, God does exist—if He made the sacred herb that we use to pray with up on the pyramids and to get lost in our own thoughts: God exists, brother.

I hurry to take a shower. I know the drug doesn't cause physical dependence but psychological, yes. Yet I prefer it to buying gringo appliances or going to the mall on the weekends.

I turn on the water in the apartment that my father bought for me three years ago. Ahhh, I love being a yuppie. I can go slumming if I want to and if not, I can hang out with the rich kids. But, oh destiny, they throw me out of both places.

I hum a little song; I pretend I'm in an apartment in New York, washing off the sweat and the day's wrinkles. I try to believe that a blonde and a brunette are waiting for me somewhere.

They'll be wearing garters and one of those bras where just the tips of the suckable nipples peek out. I pinch my own and feel a boner coming on.

I grab my dick and wave it around, it's a delicious feeling. It keeps getting bigger. "No!" I say. "I can probably find a girl in Sanborn's or at Liverpool." Of course! That's where Ylajali will be (could Ylajali be Carolina, the one who waits for me on the other side of autumn?). The women of my past have all left me through the urethra. They've abandoned me, put a knitting needle through my penis; they heated it up from the other side and I felt the beautiful taste of being abandoned. A Turkish torture.

The water feels so good running over my face, sliding down my neck and on to my stomach. Of course! That's why I don't have a girlfriend;

it's because of my pot belly. Emma Jung says uneducated women only want strong men. I should pay attention to Jung's wife and start doing some abdominals. Make myself into a goon, like the guys who go to nice parties.

I'll do it later. Now I need to get out of the shower so I can take a hit or two of pot and relieve my thirst to escape from this nightmare we call reality.

I take the towel and dry my genitals without rubbing too much; I don't want to get myself all hot again. I open the door of the bathroom and walk out naked. The curtains are open; the seventeen buildings in front of me are far enough away. No one sees me.

I grab the joint and get it going. My eyes light on a book by Elena Poniatowska that says how our great writer, Pita Amor, went to parties with only an overcoat and nothing on underneath, shouting, "I am the queen of the night!" Pita, Pita, Pita, and I without knowing what to do with my peter. What to do with this meat that goes up at a moment's notice. "I am the king of solitude," I'll shout, and I'll be Peter Amor.

I look for the same jeans I wear every day. I put on a tape of the Talking Heads: the me generation has arrived, the nineteen sixty-eights are all washed up, I think they're all alcoholics. Man, and since I was a kid I always wanted to be Che Guevara.

I decide to change the tape and put on Julio Jaramillo. "Ashes ... you know that when love has died no one holds a grudge, and if you pull away the ruins that you yourself created, you will find only ashes of what was once my love." Fuckin' Pamela, fuckin' Carolina, fuckin' broads.

I look for a shirt the TV says looks good; I'm trying to find a woman in the most racist country in the world. I put on a flowered shirt, a Hollywood boy type.

But outside, outside, oh God, so many people bogged down by poverty and misery and smog. I'm the Hollywood Boy of the Third World. Besides, there are twenty million people in this city. Oh God, who is going to read my novel? And why would they? I'm fucked. Will I be, like they say about the character in *Hunger*, 'a nomad of my own world?' I'm hungry, but all my ex-girlfriends' tits are dried up. Another mouth has finished them off.

Vroooooom

I get to the car. My flesh settles itself onto the seat, ready to live a yet-to-be-dreamed-of adventure. I put Phil Collins, Rod Stewart and el Tri in the walkman. When things are good I play rock, and when the situation gets fucked, with traffic and choking smog, I put on a Leonard Cohen tape, or maybe some José José, just to remember that I'm in love.

And I really am—I think that as I warm up the car. I'm in love with a cute little girl, but since all I talked about was jealousy and alcohol, she ran away from me. Besides, at that time there was a song by a girl group that went: "Don't tell me how to dress, don't tell me what to dream". So my little girl got her consciousness raised, became a feminist, and sent me to hell.

A sad destiny for a poet, a poet on his way to the mall determined to get the telephone numbers of a couple of blondes. Fuck it, the bad part is they're all a bunch of idiots.

I rev up to fifty miles an hour; at this point my personality transforms itself into Mad Max; I'm someone else, as I go into a curve I take a hit and think I'm He-Man. This is the best fucking part of Mexico City. Going through the streets stoned is the only viable alternative for happiness in the capital. To go around completely buzzed until some cops on the corner jump out at you and beat you with their nightsticks, screaming, "Give it up, you pothead, don't you know it's just an escape! You can't get away from this reality! Keep it up and you'll get another one where this came from!" Sheeeiit! Another smash to the head.

And if you're drunk? It's worse, then they'll shut you up in the drunk tank with a bunch of bombed bastards singing off-key. Soon their hangovers come and they start whining, then three days later it's the delirium tremens and you start to see animals crawling all over you and biting you.

I speed up to a hundred, and pretend someone's calling me on a radio transmitter. "Yes, Mike," I say. "Okay, yes Mike, here I am on the Enterprise."

I take a curve to the left and my body leans delightfully against the side of the road. A thousand men walk around inside my chest.

I escape into a delicious oblivion, turn up the music, and a police car comes up next to me. Son of a bitch, and I always said I was going to be just like Che. Shit, I've turned into an adult, I fucked up.

The other day at a party I told someone that the best age to be a guerilla is from twenty-seven to thirty-four, because you know all the strategies and your body's still functional. Holy fucking shit! I should never have said it. "Ha, ha, ha, yeah, everyone look at the revolutionary, ol' blue-eyed blond-haired Mr Credit Card!" they all join in.

"Ha, ha, ha, there you go, are you gonna start the revolution from your Mustang?"

"No, assholes," I said to them.

Then someone who talked like a faggot said, "Oh, let's talk about something else, for example, Enrique's exhibition in Amsterdam. Oh, it was wonderful!"

"Hey, what's Felipe up to, hey you, did you see we're in the Regla Rota comics this week?"

"Yeah, pretty great, huh?"

And I'm thinking, "Fucking clowns. Oh yes, dear, what a fabulous exhibition in Jalapa." Give me a break. Fucking gossip of homosexual intellectuals, I vomit on you just like I do on the clean blouse of Madame Margaret Thatcher. Assholes, I'm going to buy all your paintings so I can throw them in the garbage and you can run off and buy yourselves new cars with the money.

The truth is I didn't know if I hated human beings in general or if I was, as the intellectuals said, 'traumatized'. But the thing is, the exhibitions and the galleries left me cold. I went with the idiotic hope of finding a girl. But no, always the same face of the same jerks.

There had been a couple of interesting ones but most of them thought they were artists and that they had a direct line to God; this made them mean. They wanted everyone to look at them.

Since I'm the king of the narcissists I know all the moves; for example, you look at yourself in the reflection of a painting, act like you're looking at the painting while you secretly comb your hair, or else just dress in something outrageous.

That's why I liked doing things like putting a poblano chili down my pants. I said to myself: we all want to be seen, okay, so look at me. I'm just trying to lighten my mood up a little. Don't be scared! Aren't you intellectuals? Aren't you cool?

Jesus, what really pissed me off after going to one of those intellectual cultural get-togethers was seeing the Güero and the other guys from the block the next day. "So tell us, how many did you get?" they would ask me. "Is it true that divorced women go to those parties and they'll screw anyone?" And I'm thinking, "Jesus Christ! A bunch of assholes talking about the same thing they've talked about all their lives."

"So, tell us, how many did you get?"

"Three."

"Really?"

"Yeah, a painter, a sculptor and a girl who wanted to be Oriana Fallaci when she grew up."

"Who?"

"That doesn't matter, the thing is I did all three of them doggie style."

"No waaaaay! Really, man? Are you bullshitting us?"

"I swear."

"So who was the tightest?"

"The painter. But the sculptor was the best; she told me she was a virgin so she only wanted it in the back door."

"In the back doooooor?"

"Yep."

"What about the other one?"

"Well, the other one was a girl who said she wanted to be like Oriana Fallaci and Simone de Beauvoir when she got older, that she was looking for a man like Jean Paul Sartre who she could meet once a month and who'd leave her alone the rest of the time."

"Who are all those guys?"

"Listen, do you want to hear about the girls or the guys?"

"The girls."

"Well the truth is, the whole thing is a lie—the painter, the sculptor, and the other one. Everyone was so serious, talking about the last exhibition in Paris and shit like that. Not one of them wanted to screw. All I said to them was, "What's going on? I've come to give you some lovin', some grass and some poetry. And wham! Right there they punched me out."

"We knew you were bullshitting us!"

"I wish it weren't true. But what can you do, you know how girls are, they expect a lot of shit before they'll open their legs."

"It's fuckin' true, and then there are the ones who want you to take them to the movies. All that just so you can sleep with 'em."

"That's right. What else would you want them for?" I said.

"Nothin'."

I knew it was terrible to think that way. I should do what my friend Rogelio says: "Just shut the fuck up, you woman-hating asshole." Yeah,

yeah, I should do what my friend Rogelio says. I shouldn't be so macho. Women have feelings, too. Yeah, yeah.

"Still," I say, "some of the trashy ones are really tight."

"That's for sure."

No, no, I shouldn't say trashy ones, that's uncool, no, I should think like Rogelio does! They may be trash, but they suffer more than we do. Yeah, Rogelio's right. "Poor girls," I say, "they really suffer."

"They do not! No way! They don't suffer; they love our dicks. Like hell they suffer! The other day I was coming on to a really hot one. We had three rum and cokes and she was grabbing my dick. And it got hard in a second."

"So what happened? Did you get any?"

"No. But she gave me a blowjob. But it was a disaster, I had my father's car and I had to look for a street where I could just circle around and concentrate on coming in her mouth."

"So did you?"

"No. I was feeling so good I must have driven around for five miles. She didn't stop sucking me for a second. Besides she says she's a virgin and she wanted me to be the first one, but that she has a problem."

"What problem?" I asked him.

"She thinks she might be a lesbian, and she wants to sleep with a guy so she can make up her mind."

"Shit, man," one of his friends said. "If she sleeps with you she'll become a lesbian for sure, you'll be such a disappointment."

"Very fucking funny," the blond one said, "no, I have a special technique for controlling myself. I can go a hell of a long time without coming."

"What's your technique?" a guy who worked at the dogfights asked.

"I just think about something else."

"Shit, that's really heavy," I said.

"No, you guys," a sixteen-year-old said. "I read in a book that when you start to come the girl should press against the end of your dick, like that."

He held out his index finger and squeezed the fingertip and the nail. "You're crazy," the dogfighter said.

"No I'm not, asshole," he said in defense. "I read it the other day in a book at Sanborn's. You should learn to read, man."

"You don't even have a girlfriend. I heard that as soon as you put the rubber on you came, that you didn't even have time to get it in her."

"What are you talking about, man? I'll fuck your sister."

"Okay, cool it, assholes."

Then I remember I'm on the highway; the traffic is pretty light and I've passed eighty on automatic pilot. I read a sign that says Perisur Mall. I lower my wing flaps, start to brake, switch on my indicator, take a few turns around the lot, pull a couple more hits off the joint and park the car.

I get out of the car and there, rising up in front of me like a city in a science fiction movie, is a cluster of shops and buildings.

It's two o'clock in the afternoon and there might be a chance for a little female morsel or two.

My little girl who got her consciousness raised reading *Fem* magazine was now far away from me. Her name was Carolina. Sometimes she left messages on my machine. I really am in love with her, but since all I do is talk shit she says I bother her. I don't blame her for it, even though lately things have changed. Ever since I told her I loved her she'd rather go to her dance classes than go out with me and she says anyway she isn't ready to play the role of a typical woman. Give me a goddamn break!

She lives in Jalapa, a city of gossips, where I just got back from taking my father's ashes.

But I was in Perisur and I didn't want to think about Carolina; if I did it only would be to compare her with some super-hot piece who went by. And to say to myself, "You see, man, there are lots of great women around." She had even told me to go out with other girls. "That's it, you bastard, go ask some other girl out but stop bothering me. I'm sick of your drinking and your jealousy. Don't worry, I'm not going to sleep with anyone else, with all the dance classes I have." Carolina was so cool!

That's when I see a pair of blondes going into a store. They go over to the lingerie section and I start to get hot. The problem is if I went in there it would look pretty strange. Besides, just going up to people like that looks bad. In Perisur it's almost illegal. You can only talk to someone in your family. One family hardly ever talks to another, and if they do it's because they want something from them.

The families enter the parking lot in their little fish tanks, bickering among themselves. Once they get inside they all act like they're on a Cornflakes or Pepsi commercial. I don't understand how talking to someone you don't know has become officially in bad taste.

The blondies leave the lingerie department and I follow them. "Oh, blondies," I'm thinking, "if you only knew the orgasms I could give you!" Jesus, what ingrates. They'd rather go watch videos in some upper-class neighborhood in Chapultepec.

Sucking in my gut as much as possible, I walk up to them. "Hi, I'd like to get to know you," I say to them. "Is that all right?" They look at each other, petrified. Then, looking at me like I'm a total geek, they walk away in a huff.

I pull the same operation five or six times with some other snobs. Finally, with the still-vibrant hope of getting some flesh, I move down the socio-economic line to the salesgirls. I walk up to a women's perfume counter. "Excuse me, can you recommend a good perfume? It's for my mother." I say to a dark-skinned one.

"This one, I guess."

We talk until finally I get her telephone number. She's happy to give it to me, even though I can tell she's really tired; it's forbidden for them to sit down on the job.

Then I go up to a redhead in the clothing department and get her phone number, too.

With three new telephone numbers, and tired of sucking in my gut, I go out to the car. It's sunny out and I'm thinking things which make sense but are disjointed. I'm really enjoying myself and torturing myself with imaginary thoughts that aren't even memories, just vague bits of existence. Like that I was told I needed someone to help me correct my writing style, that Mike says you have to lie to women, that we can't say we love each other because that makes people run away, but that we have to live within ourselves so that they'll love us, that the girls who just gave me their telephone numbers have to stand up ten hours a day and aren't allowed to talk to each other or use the front entrance.

As I come up to the car I see one of those guys who hang around your parked car and then ask for money, as if they've been protecting it the whole time; this one comes up to me with a face swollen by alcohol, pissed-in pants and a crooked cap. I fished around in my pocket for a hundred pesos. The guy holds out his hand, and I give it to him. Before I get into the car I look at the giant stores around me. Whatever happened to our revolution? Did it die? Revolution for what?

I turn on the motor and drive toward my apartment, remembering the messages that are still on my answering machine; they're from Carolina, telling me she wants to show me her new world. Her new skin, her change of feeling.

Just yesterday she told me she was reading *Nuevo amor* by Salvador Novo, and *Cambio de piel* by that guy from Panama, Carlos Fuentes, I mean. Oh, Carolina is so pretty, I remember how we kissed with our eyes the very first time we saw each other. How we tenderly and shrewdly showed off our intellects so we would fall in love with each other. Useless talks, they were just part of our masks, which was only a symptom of our problems. The essential part was more eternal and timeless; we carried each other in our hearts and it settled itself into us through sex. Carolina always believed me when I told her she was the best girl I ever had in bed. She would tell me that she was just another short girl, that you could lift up a rock and find ten others. But it wasn't true, the truth was our orgasms were like threads between us that made our lives more tense, and once we got bored of each other in bed she would make me lunch, seething, telling me she couldn't tolerate being a housewife. As for me, I devoted my time to being in a bad mood, or else being jealous of her.

Our fights were as intense as our orgasms. All of this pulled us away from each other. She's happy now, and she says that when she talks to other guys I'm sitting there right next to her. Fine, if that's what she says—as long as they're not having a ménage à trois and I only get to be there in spirit, it's no problem.

The thing is, our biggest difference is that she's learned to believe in God and I never did. That made my waiting for her sad, while it made her happy. That's why I needed her. Maybe I only wanted women to love me and I confused love with needing to go to the bathroom. How disgusting.

Since I'm one of those guys who approach women with their mouths wide open, swallowing them up just to shit them out later to look for another who can satisfy the whims of the neurotic child inside us, I'm unhappy. Tremendously unhappy. I've always known that my depressive structure is unchangeable, that the only way to keep it under control is by reading something, perhaps Nietzsche: "Thinking about suicide as a persistent expectation causes us more than one sleepless night." Or maybe by walking the tightrope of mania, until I go crazy and fall into the hands of psychiatrists.

I'm back on the highway; I don't have any right to complain about anything; being a playboy of the Third World will have to be enough. I should feel happy that I live in a city with tons of fecal matter in the air. I light a joint. I breathe in its delicacy and put on the cruise control. My mind continues to wander. I remember that seven old girlfriends have gotten married, and four of them are now divorced. That Rogelio talks like a fag when he's drunk. That as soon as Mike gets inside Ocho y Medio he thinks he's a movie star. That we're all aggressive, evil clowns. Actually I'm embarrassed by Mike, Rogelio and myself. I don't know; it could be like Mike says, that I'm like a girl, always talking about symptoms. But really they depress me, my whole generation depresses me. I always wanted something different. I'm always hoping for something other than what really happens. I pass a Coca-Cola truck on the right, exit at Tacubaya, accelerate, then brake, and put on the clutch.

From far away I can see a female with lovely Cuban hips. "Want a ride?" I say to her as I drive by. She turns around to look at me but just then a truck belches out some smoke, the girl blinks it out of her eyes, and fifty cars behind me start to honk. My mind barely has time to formulate the words, "Goodbye forever, Ylajali."

Sit Doggie! Go to Veracruz, Doggie!

We have a dog named Boxca at home; when they let her out of her little room, she waits to make sure my sister's there before she'll come out to eat. That's the same thing that happens to me with women. I guess it was probably the same way with my mother, too.

I get in the lane for the highway to Puebla; I say goodbye to the terrible shroud of smog and the shitload of police and patrol cars parked at the intersections, wiping the smog out of their eyes and looking around for a puff of oxygen. But there wasn't even one fat airwave of oxygen, not one live particle, not even on the trees on Zaragoza. All their leaves were covered by a thin layer of mud, and of smoke from the cars and rich people's factories.

But after Puebla comes Jalapa, Veracruz. And that's where Carolina was. I was so desperate I had to remember she was alive just so I could tolerate a little more of life and this city. I remember the message she left on my machine: "How are you, my love? Where are you? I've been waiting for you since yesterday."

Then another message: "I'm here waiting for you with a little show" ("with a little show" meant she was wearing a black bra and a garter belt). There was a third: "I want you here with me, I want to show you the trees and the countryside, the sea, the stars. I adore you, my love." So why the fuck wouldn't I go to Jalapa to see her? But there were a couple of problems: we had been together two years, one of which I spent being jealous of her because she had slept with five other guys before me. The second problem was that we weren't friends anymore; each one said it was the other's fault that we lived five hours away from each other. Another problem was that my paranoia grew to even bigger proportions when I was there. Jalapa, like I said before, is a town full of gossips. Besides, in that city there were five dicks walking around who had been inside what I now considered my own dark, wet hole. Carolina. Carolina.

Another problem was the highway, and my constant fear of death (which is what made me write and publish) staring down a long road, sixty-five miles an hour for four hours. The whole time you know you're risking your life. I could have gone in a bus and confided in unknown drivers.

But what do you do, sitting alone in your seat, while on the other side the butt that holds all the secrets of the world is waiting for you? What could I do, knowing that Carolina would take me by the hand to the sea, to talk with all our pores open, to return to the places we had discovered together, places of hidden holes and cliffs? It was better to drive myself, to think about not crashing and to forget about Carolina's breasts, small ones like all ballerinas have. Goddamn Carolina, to think that five other bastards had sucked them. To think that she's a feminist, to think that thinking about virgins is macho on my part, to think that either I go to a small town to look for virgins or just accept that I'm fucked up. I was thinking all this at fifty miles an hour in a Caribe, "a beautiful piece of engineering" (as the commercial says).

When I finally got out of Mexico City I began to see mountains and little trees. This was and forever would be the landscape that Carolina had given me. Besides, Leopardo and my brother José Juan were in Jalapa, too. It would be great to hang out with them for a while. I'm tense and happy on my way to Jalapa, where less than a month ago we had taken my father's ashes. He who, for me and only for me, died two days ago. My father would suddenly appear in my consciousness. I thought about him only sometimes. I had planned symbolically to take his ashes to Jalapa myself, as if just being there would bring him back to life.

Ahhh. Carolina, I know you're waiting for me on the other end of the telephone; I'm going to call you so we can immediately go to a hotel, a hotel where she had probably been with one of the five guys who came before me. I remember when Rubén, a Cuban friend of mine, told me I was crazy, that being jealous of the men who came before us was a sickness. But how can you avoid it?

When I pass a Camper van I remember that one of her ex-boyfriends, the one we called the urban cowboy, had a van exactly like it and that they screwed in it in a field. "Did you do it a lot in the van?" I would ask her.

"Only three times."

"Did you come?"

"No."

Well that's okay, then, I thought. That's okay? Yeah, that's okay because I remember she took off her clothes really fast with the Urban Cowboy so he'd put it in, get it over with and stop bothering her. Because Carolina swore she'd loved only me, that her life went from bi-dimensional to tri-dimensional when she met me. I have to make do with that.

I come to Perote, only forty minutes to Jalapa. The road is all curves, a descent into fog. There are some trees around here that my father planted forty years ago. Are they still there?

The fog makes it difficult to see, cars are going off the road all over the place. One has a good opportunity to lose one's life, but if Carolina was waiting for me "on the other side of autumn", what did I care? She says it into my ear, too bad it's only on the telephone. But now she'll say it and I'll kiss her and kiss her and kiss her, I'll look for a kiss never given before by anybody. I'll get one straight from God or from the Devil, but it will be a first for her.

I wasn't even the first one to give it to her in the ass. I remember that at the beginning the idea seemed strange to her, but after she put some saliva and some cream on it, her sphincter settled itself down on my penis .... Oooooooh. A goddamn curve, the fog and a trailer with the lights turned off.

I remember that when I was in Jalapa I read *Original Sin*, about the life of Anthony Quinn, and that at the end the most horrifying of his traumas was to have been the second man to screw his wife.

Feminists say language is sexist. For example, calling an actor an actress. But now language is feminist; all you have to do is announce at some pseudo-intellectual gathering that you're looking for a virgin and they'll kick you out for being a reactionary.

Being a feminist is good, being macho is bad, of course; that's why I shouldn't think about the five who have already been all over Carolina (six, counting me). I remember one time we were in bed and I recognized in myself some gestures and movements that were just like my father's. Okay, that makes it seven. Though it would be eight, if you think about

Carolina's father. We call him Hosco. He really added to my paranoia, because even though he hadn't had her sexually, he represented Order, the Great Other, the "most powerful signifier" as the Lacanians would say. "Castration" to the Freudians. "The Boss" to the Marxists. Anyway, The Hoscos are the ones who give the orders, whether on a conscious or unconscious level. Do you feel like going to the park to make out with your girlfriend? You can't! She'll feel the Hosco's presence and tell you she has to go home to make lunch. Of course when she makes lunch for *you* she'll say you're sexist, or that you're just using her. Ah, but the minute the Hosco asks them to go somewhere, they comply with the letter of the law. There's no human power able to convince them that it would be better to go to a motel and roll around in the delicious filth of sex. No, and do you know why? Because they love the Hosco more. Their response to your amatory angst will be: "I just HAVE TO go with my father." If you're not stupid you'll realize that fighting this HAVE TO is useless. And in case she decides to go with you, the Hosco will hover around like a ghost and will stop her from having an orgasm, or else she won't want to fuck at all. And in case she tells the Hosco to go to hell and she has a great time with you, in no more than five years the Hosco will snap his fingers and she'll go running to him, inventing some reason why she has to go; see, there's some very interesting master's program that happens to be exactly where the Hosco lives. The Holy Saint of Castration. The Lord who created the laws that obsessive Hoscos always follow. The man of the flaccid dick who packs a rock-hard pistol.

A goddamn monster-size truck is trying to pass me from behind. Could it be Hosco? Will he fuck me, too, plunging into me with his terrifying double-edged sword? Will he hurt my poor ass, shit-tired and tired of shitting? I move to the side and the truck passes, brushing the side of my car.

Happy to still be alive, I take out a joint. A Jewish friend of mine who we call the Pot Queen gave it to me. It's a fat, delicious joint, ready for my Cricket lighter to illuminate the dense fog that makes me love my solitude. I light it, drinking in the colostral nectar of the ever-flowing nipples of Olympian goddesses.

I remember I'm writing this novel and that I told myself I'd finish it in twenty-eight days. Twenty-eight days, the menstrual cycle of a woman who bathes me in her blood. Every twenty-eight days women get mad at us. Neglect to give them a child and it's fuck off. The missing object of desire, Freud would say. Plus, ever since my last book came out women have rejected me; they say I'm too dirty. "Ewww, how could you call a book *Baby, Do Me a Favor and Take off Your Underpants*?" If you whistle at a woman on the street, or you say something to her like, "What beautiful eyes! See you later, darling, cutie-pie!" they feel flattered. But be careful, if you happen to say, "Let's do it doggie style, mama!" or "You're a great fuck!" or "I'll suck them, so you can rest a little!" they'll think you're evil. They live in error inside their own repression. The truth is the ones who talk about beautiful eyes turn out to be jerks; they're the type who say you should treat a woman "like a rose petal". But they forget about the thorns.

But this is supposed to be a novel; the thing is the pot makes my mind wander all over the place. Why does the government burn all the Mary Jane? She's the only good woman humanity has given us. "Smoke grass and life will transform itself." Or maybe it's like Nietzsche said: "Man longs for the sweetness of woman, but she is a cat who only feigns her sweetness." I look out at the trees; my gaze is a laser beam that cuts through the fog, and the forest, invaded by my cold stare, becomes even greener. I feel good, very good, because I am going to see Carolina, Leopardo and José Juan. I watch a truck go by filled with workers. "Poor devils!" I say. "They don't have a Carolina waiting for them."

Telephone Style

I get to Jalapa and the first thing I do is look out my petroleum-powered spaceship for a telephone. I wanted to find one as soon as possible. Fuck this traffic; these assholes in front of me are going so slow. A telephone! Carolina, my love, where are you? "What sadness lengthens your hours?" a friend of Shakespeare's Romeo asks him. He answers, "Not having that which, having makes them short."

I finally find a place to park and go into the Parroquia cafe. Nervously, I stick a coin in the pay phone. It rings once; Carolina must be far away from the phone. Then it rings twice, three times, then four. I just hope Hosco doesn't answer. Ring ring ring and I'm wrung out.

Why isn't Carolina there? I'm sure I left a message with her friend that I would call at five o'clock, and it was five o'clock now. I turn around to look at the people in the cafe. Tired intellectuals, most of them posers who, whenever they see me drunk, edge away in fear, then run off to read Malcolm Lowry or Dylan Thomas.

What would happen if just when I'm sitting here thinking this she comes into the cafe and sits down right next to the telephone? No, it would be too much of a coincidence. I'll wait one more minute, no, five minutes. I walk out onto the street; the yuppies go by in their cars, their stereos blasting. A man without legs pushes himself along on a little cart.

After four minutes I go back into the cafe. I see someone I know and don't like. It's a guy with the face of a true asshole. I've been coming to Jalapa for more than twenty years and for twenty years I've been seeing his stupid face. How miserable it is to live in this hell where every day we have to see people we can't stand!

I don't know if he's looking at me 'cause he wants a fight or if it's because he saw my last book, or if he thinks I'm just another rich boy from Jalapa. I look at his arms, bare, sinewy, and strong.

I call Carolina again, it rings two three four five six seven eight nine ten knockout. I hang up. My God! Where is she? Where is the skin that covers like a blanket a neurotic and poetic young boy?

I look again at the sinewy guy I don't like. I leave the cafe and stop in the street. And if this jerk inside was the guy Carolina lived with for three months? Of the five guys she slept with before me there are three I've never seen.

And what if he knows I'm Carolina's boyfriend and I don't know he's an ex? And what if he attacks me from behind for being one who got the prize? I go back into the cafe. If I were a dog the whole world would see my tail between my legs; the atmosphere is hostile. Hosco might be around here, or Charrurris, or the short Marxist. He was a guy who dressed like a pop-star and read Marx. Carolina told me she only slept with him two times a week, and that they did it with the light turned off.

This did nothing for my nerves. "But this guy, was his bigger than mine?" I asked her, embarrassed.

"No," she said, but my question annoyed her.

"Listen," I went on, "was he always on top or did you do it in other positions?"

"No, he was always on top."

"Well," I thought, "thank God for that."

But this guy inside the cafe could have been the live-in boyfriend. I mean the one she lived with for three months.

One time Carolina was lying in bed next to me with one breast sticking out of the covers. And she told me that the live-in one was a prude, always telling her to "cover yourself up". So what did that mean? Well, it meant that Carolina used to lie in bed with her breasts hanging out after screwing. What did it matter if you had your breasts out in the open or if you were modest, if the guy had already rubbed and sucked them with his disgusting tongue?

I feel a dizzy spell coming on, and I start walking towards Juárez Park. I'd have to wait, it would be better to try to waste some time and stop thinking about Carolina on the other end of the fucking goddamn piece of shit telephone.

On the way I see a guy in a muscle shirt, shoulders bared. He's more or less the same age as the pop-Marxist who used to screw Carolina. But it doesn't matter; she didn't always come when they screwed. Besides, Carolina clearly explained to me that one thrust of my cock was like an orgasm with all the other five guys put together. As I already explained, I taught her the art of tri-dimensionality.

One time I asked her, "If the orgasms you have with me are one hundred, how would you rate the ones with your ex-boyfriends?"

"Some around twenty, others thirty."

"Jesus. That high?"

"Well," she said, holding me, "some were less than twenty."

"But you still did it with them."

"It was as if I didn't."

"So why did you bother?"

"It makes me nervous to masturbate."

"Did you used to think of anyone when you masturbated?"

"Yes, but he didn't have a face."

"That's because it was me."

Another kid goes by who could be a friend of the sinewy asshole. Besides, what did it matter if she came or not? The sad truth was, a whole line of bastards had enjoyed themselves with Carolina's ass. They had pawed at it, not knowing that someday it'd be mine. Just playing a game to wound me.

No, no, no. I have to remember Rogelio. "Gimme a goddamn break.

You treat women like your own private property. You're sick." He always criticized me.

"Maybe, but socialists get jealous, too. Can't you see we all come from the same place—a fuck? That's right—the father took our place."

Yes, yes, yes, I must think like Rogelio thinks, I can't be so Victorian. I am truly sick. After half an hour, I go back to call again. Hosco answers. "No, she's not here." I hang up.

I leave again to go to the park, only now I'm even more shaken up, and my nerves get mixed up with my fear; I feel my balls stuck to my body with such force that they pull on my sphincter and I know that any minute I'll shit from pure fright and solitude. Fuckin' Carolina, why did she tell me to come here? I can't call again so soon since Hosco's sitting right next to the telephone.

I keep walking and walking and then I see Zoé. He's a thin guy with long hair who loves to get high. "What's goin' on?" he says.

"Nothin', just trying to get away from the smog," I answer. I want to avoid telling him I'm here to see Carolina, since I have no idea where she is or how she'll act when she sees me.

"So you've escaped from ol' Distrito Federal."

"Yep," I say. "I was pacing around my apartment, smoking one cigarette after another, then I called Rogelio to see if he had any ideas and he told me I should pull a Mad Max, leave Mexico City for Jalapa and then turn around and go back to Mexico City and just keep going back and forth until I'm out of my fucking head. You see, that's the only way Mad Max could calm down. What about you?" I asked him. "Got a joint?"

"Nah. Hey, guess who I saw. Your girlfriend."

At that moment I feel my blood go cold. I prepare myself for the worst possible news—who did he see her with? Where? In which hotel? My heart rises up into my throat, I'm about to cry, I'm about to shit in my pants. Finally I say, my voice shaking, "Oh yeah? Where?"

"In La Atasca. That place has gotten pretty good lately."

I'm sure the world is going to plunge out of orbit, they've finally dropped the bomb, I want to cry, to run to Carolina and scream at her, "So what the fuck were you doing having fun at La Atasca while I was wandering around drunk and banging my head against the wall because you weren't with me?"

At the edge of the darkest abyss, but not wanting to appear jealous, I say, "I'm sure she was with her friends."

"Yeah, a group of girls who are into dance and aerobics."

I know those kind of girls. Not the same ones, but I knew the attitude. They're almost always beautiful, and good, they all have a true love, and I was Carolina's.

Zoé and I walked around Jalapa; I thought every woman I saw was Carolina, I wanted her so bad. I had even forgotten about Ylajali, the unknown goddess who was waiting for me. I was so happy I was going to see Carolina that I confused her with Ylajali. I even remember I had brought a tape of Billie Holliday that we listened to when we first met.

The time went by, my skin felt sore and tender from waiting so long; it was like a tree with thin bark being scraped away by sadistic children. A minute went by and I said to myself, "She must be home by now." I asked Zoé twice to call and ask to speak to her. Her father answered.

My God! I had driven almost three hundred miles to feel the embrace that would become my only reason for existence—the breath of a woman.

As we walked we passed a house where my father lived when he was young. From where we were you could see a well and the entrance to the rooms. I thought I should cry, but I didn't. The house was as unknown to me as my own infancy; as much as I tried to visualize it, I could only remember it from photos of when I was small. My father had played as a boy in that house, and now he was no longer here. I would have liked him to be around so I could tell him about Carolina, but why? He would only say, “You’re not crying for your muse but for a mouse.” I got an idea and went with Zoé to look for her in the club where she practiced dance with her friends. We got there and there were small groups of women with sweat pants, tights, leotards, and pounds and pounds of ego.

Yeah, I thought, remembering Nietzsche: “How lovely that there are creatures with their heads full of dance, caprices and clothing.” But none of them was Carolina.

If I had bought her roses they would have wilted; that’s why I didn’t, I knew they’d wilt. I asked Zoé: “Hey, am I too much of a wimp with Carolina?”

“When I was in love I was, too,” he said.

Embarrassed by my own craziness and my wild goose chase, I gave him a ride downtown to go hang out with his buddies. “See ya, Zoé, see if you can get some pot.” I could barely speak; I was flattened by my anxiety and feelings of abandonment. He got out of the car.

I parked on a street where I imagined I’d find her; two or three pretty women walked by. Even if one of them were Ylajali it wouldn’t matter, I would look and keep looking for Carolina, for her gaze, her voice, her arms.

I saw someone who looked like her; she was talking and laughing with some guy. Besides just being jealous, now I felt envious. Why wasn’t I with her right now? I decided I would keep walking to kill some time; I watched my feet and with every step I counted one second; my eyes were on my shoes, I was almost crying, a constant and continuing oppression tightened my throat. There was neither time nor space, only waiting; it was so awful it made me ask someone for the time every five minutes. Anxious, and barely realizing it, I reached another telephone; by now it was nine o’clock. Her father answered. “I already told you she isn’t here, now please stop calling.”

“Thank you, sir.” I hung up.

I didn’t know what to do. It made me want to have a drink, but after the last time I was afraid of the consequences; besides, it would only make Carolina happy. For a year she's been saying to me, "Go ahead, get drunk! What you sow, you reap: and that's hatred."

I thought the best thing to do would be to cry for my father, but at that moment I just didn't feel like it. It would have made more sense to cry for him, for death, for something concrete, for a hard gravestone.

Not being able to cry for my father made me even more nervous. I went back to the car to look for a joint. I breathed in the smoke, hoping to calm down, but instead I felt worse. I searched through my bag for some Valium that would put me to sleep until a reasonable time that Carolina might get home, but I didn't find any. I made my hands into fists and began to beat against the steering wheel. Every time I punched it a second went by in which Carolina would be getting home. I felt what I was doing was stupid and useless. I started the motor and went to my parents' house; well, my mother's, as my father, as I said before, now inhabited the concrete world: an urn of ashes.

When I got home my brother was standing in the doorway, pissed off about something. He already knew I was coming. "Hi," he said, furious, like all older brothers. I went into the house; Leopardo was there studying an English-Spanish dictionary; he and my brother were going after some gringas at the time. I asked him: "What's wrong with José Juan?"

"It's just that you interrupted his privacy."

"It's my house too."

I went into the living room. I walked up to him as you would to pet a strange cat. "What's goin' on?" I said. "Are you pissed about something?"

"I just can't believe it!" he was almost screaming. "You're always fucking with me. I've had six shitty months and the day I start to feel better, you show up."

The house was quiet; if you could have heard the hate he was aiming my way, we would have all gone deaf. "I'm waiting for Carolina to get home. But I'll go to a hotel." That calmed him down a little. But just a little—he knew that my being born after him had destroyed him in a way. I thought about three-year-old children who poke out the two-year-olds' eyes.

Oh God! I was alone. Without Carolina, with a brother who spit in my face, with my father dead. My mother and my therapist were in Mexico City. What was missing with my therapist was, according to the Lacanians, my 'a' object, which, according to the Freudians, was the cause of my anxiety, brought on by the neurosis of transference. According to me, he was a person who listened to me and made me feel something.

And my mother? At that exact moment she called on the phone, imploring me as if I were God himself, "Please don't fight with your brother!"

I went to find refuge in my solitude; there was nothing else to do. I exchanged two or three words with Leopardo, preferring not to talk for too long because it would only be about the same thing: waiting. And waiting was getting more and more tortuous.

My brother left the house. Being with Leopardo made me think about Truman Capote, who said that he could only talk about his life with two or three people; everything else was just alternating monologues. I called Carolina's house again. She answered. "What happened? I've been waiting for you for five hours," I said.

"I didn't know you were coming. I have to go with my mother; she's giving an exam. I'll see you in an hour."

During that hour I felt newly alive, the feeling of splinters sticking into my skin disappeared. It was a concrete time to wait; she would be here in one hour. My brother came back with a German girl.

Later another guy showed up with some Romanian broad. This guy had read my poetry and gushed over it while I sat stationed by the window waiting for Carolina's headlights. An hour went by and she didn't arrive. I started to feel dead, dried-up flakes of skin all over me; I say dead not to be redundant but to describe the condition of my heart.

A minute went by, then two, three, five, thirty, forty, another hour. Everyone else got ready to go out to a party.

I stayed alone in the empty house. I was bothered by the absence of my father. I remember once José Juan and I were arguing and he told me that I was the one who had let my father die. I wasn't with him because I had gone to be with Carolina. I left him to rot alone so I could be with Carolina's ass.

That's when she got there.

What the Fuuuuck?

And now what? And then what? There on the surface of my skin lay seven dead hours. My nerves, destroyed by waiting, were restless and bothered.

I leaned out the window. She was in her father's Ford. When I saw her I felt profoundly sad for myself. How can such a small being in the constellations provoke in my head from millions of years of evolution these desires to destroy my own veins and my life?

I felt like bawling her out for being late; an imperious necessity to do it made the blood pound in my ears.

I went outside. I walked up to her in order to kiss her; since she hadn't gotten out of the car and it was dark, I stuck my head in the window, brushed her cheek with my lips and felt my heart beginning to beat again. But when I pulled my head back it felt like I wasn't doing the right thing—I should nag her a little. Those seven hours of waiting were racing around in my body, even my penis was in a sadistic and vulgar mood: it refused to become erect.

I thought about the night around us, the shadows of the pure and vigilant trees, the crickets, the fireflies, life itself. "Yes!" I thought to myself, "I should be happy with life, that's what's normal, now breathe deeply." I lit a cigarette.

She got out of the car. I could tell immediately; it was a different Carolina. This Carolina was so full of life that she no longer belonged to me. She was wearing a few different-sized sweaters, a scarf, four bracelets on her left hand, two on the right and a few rings. When she lived with me she only wore one bracelet; now she had more earrings, she was restless, she knew beforehand that I had been waiting and that it bugged me to wait. I remembered that a friend told me that women are like loose threads, bits of fluff from a sweater that anchor themselves on any conversation or shoe store window around. "Hi!" she said. "Why aren't you hugging me?"

"Because I'm sick," I thought. But I hugged her anyway. I felt the arteries of our hearts join together until they produced a tender and erotic transfusion. Just then I let her go and a monster who was holding me hostage said to her, "Why did you make me wait?"

"I told you my friend never told me you were coming."

I held her away from me so I could ask her what I wanted: "Are you coming back to Mexico City? I'll take a week."

"I can't just leave everything."

"Not even a week?"

"No, but if you want I'll come down on Sunday."

"It's Thursday now, so you want me to leave tomorrow?"

"I have some things to do here."

"Like what?"

"We're going out to the indigenous community."

Carolina also wanted to be Che Guevara when she was a teenager. "We're going to be the ones to make the revolution!" we had told each other.

"Why are you going there? Right there are six presidents meeting, they're all anti-Reagan, there's nothing for us to do."

"But there is for me. You only go out there for the meals, and so you can laze around all day."

Yep, a different Carolina.

"I don't want a slave or a revolutionary either, I want a mate," I said.

"But always doesn't mean every day, we can see each other five minutes and they'll be like an eternity. Besides, remember what Erich Fromm said: 'Love is the child of freedom.' And he based his theories on Marx, on Marx, do you hear me?"

"Yeah, but who do you think took care of Marx's kids and changed their diapers?"

"Aha! That's what you want from me; well, I refuse to fall into the typical system of woman's oppression."

"All I'm asking for is a week, and that you don't stand me up again."

"If you behave yourself, stop drinking and promise not to be jealous, then maybe I'll decide to live with you."

"I always try to behave myself. I've tried to stop talking about Schopenhauer and other machos because I know it bothers you. I'm going to AA even though it's a bore. I haven't acted jealous, and now you're the one who has to take Valium to get to sleep because you feel so anxious and guilty without knowing why."

"Well, yeah, but I'm not going to stop doing my own things."

It was another Carolina; the mother she was to me would never be back. She was a feminist now; she had filled her head with authors who told women to abandon men in order to free themselves, authors who I had first shown her when we still talked about things like that. I read them to her and she commented on them, but I never imagined that, like a monster of science fiction, she would feed herself off them to engender this terrible being. "Okay," she said, "let's forget it." She lifted up her skirt, showing me her legs engulfed by the night. A black leotard formed a V from where a few loose pubic hairs peeked out. I immediately felt a tug on my dick. But instead of feeling excited, I felt contemptuous. She didn't know that I had to provoke this tug and this excitement all by myself in my apartment in Mexico City three times a week. My own mirror, full of dust and masturbation, lived on, desolately, foolish, shattered and bringing bad luck. "You know what?" I told her, lighting another cigarette with the stub I still had left. "Know what? I'm sick of masturbating! Sick of it!"

She pulled down her skirt and looked at me coolly. "I already told you, you can go out with other girls."

"Other girls? I'm going to change a breast for a pacifier? Fuck other girls! I AM IN LOVE WITH YOU! Do you hear me? With you!"

"Oh yeah? And what about Pamela? Didn't you tell me you were never going to stop loving her?"

"Pamela's married to an engineer."

"So what? That's probably a relief to you."

"Don't you love me anymore?" I asked her, like a man who waits for a ship that is sinking in the distance and will probably never arrive.

"Yes I love you, but not in the way you love me."

I had heard this comment so many times in my life I thought I should be put away right then.

"Oh yeah? And how do you all love, you who wake up to go running in the mornings? You who love apples for breakfast instead of smoking, and who work nine to five? How do you love?"

"I already told you. 'Love is the child of freedom.'"

I felt my throat tighten. I swallowed, trying to feel like the hero of a movie; I wanted to see if this narcissistic pose would lighten things up a little. I walked to the corner with a cigarette for company. From there you could glimpse a dark area with a fig tree. A tree where my father wanted his ashes to be buried: turned out it was prohibited because of questions of contamination. Even at the border you need a special permit to bring over ashes. I kept thinking about my father. I wanted him to be with me so he would talk badly about women. Carolina had stayed fifty feet behind me. From the fig tree I looked over at her, doing a classical dance, in the night. This pissed me off even more; she wanted me to love her for her dance classes and for her activities when she was away from me. Three days later I would be back in Mexico City. A dirty cloud of smog and solitude would shit down on my face. And there she was, dancing, with the histrionic look of all the ballerinas who have gone through my life. A look that says they know they're being looked at. While she concentrated on pointing the line of her arm towards the sky and rising up on one leg, I starting feeling sorry for her, and hatred for myself. The truth is I was the monster, the monster of jealousy and drink. She had only come to lick her wounds in front of the mirror of a dance studio.

But what could I do? I loved her and hated her at the same time. This was nothing new; it seemed like something indissoluble, a knot of three vise-like circles—madness, desire, and anxiety, that fall together to create longing.

I thought about sex; I preferred to think about it than to feel it. I knew that if we went to a hotel I'd feel five times more alone then when I had come. Why the fuck had I come to Jalapa? I thought that it was symbolically to bring my father's ashes, but this was a useless interpretation.

I preferred to deal with the pain of displeasure and I went over to hug her. She held me lovingly, rubbing her cold, peachy cheeks over my beard and my sideburns. I kissed her on the forehead as if it held some special significance. It was sealing our farewell. That kiss on the forehead was as quick as God's wink.

"Let's go to a hotel!" I said to her.

"Okay, but let me go to the bathroom first, I'm peeing in my pants," she said. She went into the bathroom of my house.

Night

While she was in the bathroom I lit a joint. I felt like the drug was my only salvation, and actually, it was. Marijuana would never abandon me, and she would. I remembered when we lived together and would spend days in bed eating fish with garlic, and fruit, and sweets.

Goodbye to all that. Now my girlfriend was a feminist and I had to play the liberal: tolerate the whole feminist thing that I went through when I was in high school, without a girlfriend. Now, even though I believed in it, I hated it and I made fun of it, I felt that it was an evil dogma. I felt like a sexist pig and a retro bore at the same time.

And what could I do when she wasn't around? Read *Fem* magazine? Continue masturbating until blood came out of my urethra? Look for a dirty baby bottle in place of a cushiony mother? What should I do? Work? At what? All work was death to me; the only thing that relieved my boredom was to write, write, write all day until my spine began splintering and bleeding, not stopping to cry or to breathe, simply to write and write until, at last and somehow, Carolina would be the same as before and the unknown fruits that she spoke of, that she whispered of, would return. The ones she uses to abandon me stay with me through all my lonely, overstimulated nights. Carolina, when was it that you died?

She comes out of the bathroom. I watch her movements objectively, my brain registering it like a camera. My unconscious and my subconscious knew this would be our last night, that later we would fight, that she would marry someone else, or, like a liberated woman, would live in 'free union' with some intellectual of Jalapa. My conscious faintly perceived that this was our last night. Meanwhile, I say to myself, I must believe that the war of the sexes will liberate her from the monster that has a hold on her and that she'll come back with me for a week. Just one fucking week.

I want to find some magic phrase that will make her say to me, "Let's go spend a week together, right now." But everything is bullshit and fantasy; reality is something else, something cruder. She picks up her bag. "Let's go;" she says, "tomorrow I have to go somewhere with my mother at six a.m."

This means she'll wake me up to tell me she's leaving and I'll end up lying in a bed in some stupid motel until she comes back; I know she'll keep me waiting for hours. It'll be the same scene as today: walking like a somnambulist across my own anxiety, planning a new strategy to find her on the phone by way of Hosco, and all the other fucking goddamned delightful shit of my existence. "Why do you have to leave in the morning?" I ask her.

"I'll be back by eleven," she says.

"If you've forgotten, you've kept me waiting approximately fifteen times without showing up."

"So let's not go to a hotel, let's not go anywhere."

She walked toward the door of the house. I knew she knew that she had me by the balls and by my loneliness. But even knowing she was leaving a dead man in that house, she opened the door and walked towards the car. I followed her as if she were someone else. Playing the fool, I said, "Um, okay, what hotel do you want to go to?"

"That's all you want from me, isn't it?" She raised her skirt, pissed off and showing me her legs. "This is what you want! A hole! So, what are you waiting for, take it, but you'll never see me again."

"Relax, take it easy."

We were the most mortal enemies on earth. Abel and Cain in male and female form. Her pussy was the donkey's jawbone that she would use to kill me. I had no chance to save myself—only by killing her—and that solution seemed like such a tacky detective story that it was useless; besides I shouldn't do it, the idea was for her not to leave me. All I could do was insult her for what she was doing, to tell her that all dancers were narcissistic man-eaters with dried up tits.

She got mad again and I then stopped insulting her. I was so suspicious of her that I couldn't even treat her well; I knew that flattering her and acting like her lapdog would cause me more pain when she sent me to hell.

I had already felt ridiculous too many times.

I decided to shut up. I would accept her pussy, the donkey's jawbone she would use to kill me with, to send me once again to the death of abandonment. She'd do it in an instant—a mere shutter-click of God. I had been bad, jealous and a drunk. I should accept my punishment and die, suffocating in her forest of pubic hair like a child strangled by the umbilical cord of its mother.

Hotel

I looked for the hotel, breathing silently and waiting for my silence to make her feel alone and to reach out to me.

But the silence—or at least the silence you could hear in between the gear changes of the Ford—was impenetrable and full of tricks. It only made me realize that in fact, I was not yet in Jalapa. I felt her looking at me like I was a stack of photos she was seeing for the thirtieth time. Besides, now Jalapa belonged to her; to her and her body. It was no longer the Jalapa of my past and present family, it was a city totally occupied by her. We passed a cafe where I imagined Carolina losing her virginity ten years ago.

"My first time?" I remember her telling me. "Well, I was about seventeen years old and I was in this cafe. I saw a guy I liked the looks of, I didn't think he was from around here and I thought I'd never see him again. I stared at him until he sat down next to me, and I started to talk about sexual liberation until he suggested we go to a hotel that afternoon. But I didn't enjoy it, I was too afraid he'd know I was a virgin."

I never knew which cafe she was talking about, but I always believed it was the one with big windows where they sold salami and sausage baguettes.

I remember I immediately christened that first guy in her life 'The No-Name'. A guy who went back to look for her three days after deflowering her and to whom she said no, no more, it was just for that one time. She never went out with him again. This incident caused a hole in my spirit. The whole thing seemed so slutty and so arrogant that for a minute I thought I was hanging out with a sleazy hooker.

I kept torturing myself in silence. I looked at the hills on the streets in fear. They were filled with intrigue and cunning. Everyone knew everything about everyone. People talked about her, said she organized orgies, that she slept with three men at once and that she was a drug addict. What they said about me was that I was an alcoholic, a pothead, a homosexual, a pervert, a sadomasochist and a party-crasher.

This very thing is what made us love each other; when we met we felt like outsiders to all the Jalapa shit. We were self-marginalized and in love with this conviction; that's why we made love the first time we went out.

Everything was beautiful then; since I was still courting her I behaved like a typical liberal, grinning like an idiot.

After two months I began to realize she was fickle; she swore to me that with her other boyfriends she had waited two months before going to bed with them. And I realized that I was sick with jealousy. I realized that in my mother's eyes, and in my own, women who weren't virgins were whores. There was no way out of it; I was resentfully sitting in a corner of a dark, cold house full of Victorian moralism. I tried to save myself through my friends and the advice of non-jealous people, but it was too late; I discovered that jealousy isn't a thought, but rather an ache.

She parks her car next to a hotel. "Let's go where we went last time," she says.

"Great."

I got out of the car without kissing her. I tried to think about Pamela and the undying love she professed for me. Too bad she was with the engineer now. Fucking hell.

Not kissing her, and then watching her following me into the hotel, I imagined I was one of the ex-boyfriends she said she never really loved. She was going to a hotel with me not out of love, but out of obligation, and to finally realize her guilt-ridden masturbation fantasy: to get herself a faceless fuck.

A fifty-year old man was watching a portable TV. It was midnight. "Do you have a room for two people?"

"Two beds or one?" he asked. "We're married," I answered, thinking he had asked just to be morbid. I felt like crying and telling the man that it wasn't true, that we weren't married and that tomorrow we would separate forever, that we hadn't said it but we knew it would happen that way, and we were just waiting for one last orgasm. I felt lightheaded at the whole situation.

Carolina was standing next to me without touching me. She looked at some plastic flowers and I looked at her with her clothes, bracelets and earrings. I had a million fetishes. I was charged up by so much femininity and mirrors. It was too heavy; I didn't know how to lighten it up and go back to the time "when we were happy", to the times of fish with garlic, of fruit and candy.

I barely realized that I'd paid and we were going toward the room. Ours was number sixteen. We went in and then she said, "I'm exhausted. My dance class was really hard today." She lay down, tired, and I lay down too, drained from thinking so much. I told her I loved her. That I didn't want her to say anything. That she shouldn't tell me all about her new knowledge of the Bible and other philosophies of love, but just that I loved her.

This annoyed her. She started to talk about who knows what philosophy of love. She was bugged because I tried to shut her up, saying that we should let love possess us. But telling her to be quiet was macho behavior, according to her. She went on about it for a few minutes. They were minutes of hatred; knowing that she was going to leave early and wasn't going to give me even a week of her existence made my balls boil.

Then she lowered her hand and began to caress my penis. It immediately got erect. I took it out of my pants and watched how her hand moved up and down mechanically, like she was milking a cow.

I got up on one arm and saw that someone had scratched little hearts into the paint on the headboard, and written the words, "Alejandro and Gabriela made love here." Then, like a man ready to risk everything on the roulette, I bet my words like a chip: "Why don't we make a heart to say that you and I were here together?"

"God, how corny," she answered.

With that I lost the bet, and saw that two years of a relationship had been for nothing. There was no more time or space, only a mediocre writer with a stiff prick and a mediocre ballerina milking me with her hand.

I was annoyed, but I tried not to show it when I got up to go to the bathroom. When I turned on the light a giant cockroach ran to hide under the sink. I stood in front of the sink, wanting to cry and to pee. I couldn't do either. If I cried she would take advantage of me and present me with the final blow—leaving me without her pussy. I had to wait for my erection to go down a little; now and then I pushed on the head, trying to get it to point towards the toilet, but the more I touched it the harder it got. Then I tried to think about other things besides sex and women. I remembered once when I was drunk I wanted to kill myself with gas, but that I had been so afraid to expose myself even one minute to the gas, and I didn't know where this instinct toward life came from. My dick was loosening up until finally it let the urine out and I began to piss in streams. It went down some more, and then I let loose a thick, yellow, bubbly stream.

When I left the bathroom I had a terrible shock: I didn't recognize this hotel. The room either. Maybe she had been here with someone else and thought it was me. I couldn't resist the temptation and I asked her, "Is this where we came last time?"

"Yes," she answered, knowing what I was thinking. I got back into bed with her, I held her, I looked at her brown eyes, her painted mouth, her even teeth. I loved it all. "I love you," I said. "I know you don't believe me, but I love you."

This little spark brought her back to life. "Hello!" she said, recognizing me all over again as her true love. That was when she went down to my cock and put it in her mouth. She started to suck it all the way to the root, my pubic hair covering her face like a moustache. Then she hugged me again. "I love you, too," she said.

Then I pulled myself completely away from her; I moved back so she wouldn't even feel our clothes touching. She took off her jacket, her sweater and her scarf; all she had on was a leotard and her skirt. I looked around the still unfamiliar room. I pulled down the shoulders of her leotard; she didn't resist me at all. In that moment I felt a great sadness. Of course! She had stripped for other guys in this same hotel! And so what? What was she giving me, then? Conversation? No. Company? Only for a while. Love? Long distance. Pleasure? Like any other hole.

I saw her face illuminated by the light from the bathroom. It was the face of a hypocrite, like that of a hooker about to fulfill her end of the deal. Worse than that. A hooker would have dared to put her name and mine on the headboard of the bed. I felt so disgusted by my thoughts and her past that I had to look at the ceiling, making an effort not to run out and kill someone. She didn't come close to me; she could have easily fallen asleep until the internal and obsessive alarm woke her up to go with her mother at five in the morning without feeling the need to make love. It was because she didn't love me anymore, or at least not the way I loved her.

I began to lick her light pink nipples, they got erect and she started to moan. She also started to touch my nipples with the point of a fingernail. I got hard again. I told her I wanted to go down on her, that I wanted to kiss her clitoris as if it were the tip of her tongue. "But I took two dance classes today and I haven't taken a shower," she said.

"It doesn't matter."

"I'd rather you didn't."

We kissed each other as if pulling fish from the sea; she seemed to be really hot. Little bits of leftover love were still in her spirit and I got them out with my tongue, licking at all the edges: the corners of her eyes, her belly button, her ears, her ass. I began to stroke her labia minora with my gland; they were wet and it went in easily. "I want it inside me, now. I haven't masturbated since we last saw each other," she said.

"Do you want me to put on a rubber?"

"No, it's okay, I'm using something."

Since she wasn't in love with me I didn't want a baby either, and I believed her. I put it deep inside her. "More, more, deeper," she was screaming and moaning. I thrust it in and out, trying to infuse it with all the love I could. It was my best shot. I fought not to come yet and lose everything. Love helped me hold it in and stay for a while, in and out, enjoying it, thinking that the world was charged with neutrons, that the revolution had died but that we were in that moment alone and inseparable.

Then, plaintive and excited, she begged, "Give it to me doggie style!" I pulled her up by the waist, turned her over, and put her at the edge of the bed. She got on all fours, arching her back so her ass was higher. I penetrated her with anxiety and desire. "I love you, I love you. I've never loved anyone else. Pinch my ass. Pinch it!" she was saying. I pinched her furiously. "Harder!" she screamed. Then she pulled at me so I'd climb on top of her. She rubbed some saliva on her sphincter and began to put it in the other way, that is to say, in her ass.

She stuck it in her by slowly lowering herself down on me. "This is how you convince me," she said, "this is what makes me feel like dropping everything and being your slave! I want to lick your balls for a lifetime!" She rode me faster and faster until I couldn't stand it anymore and I came, Carolina meeting me with a sublime anal orgasm.

Afterward she said she was cold and asked me to cover her. When she fell asleep I kissed her tenderly, running over her body with my lips as if I were running over an entire life on her one skin. I knew this was our last night so I dedicated myself to going over her skin with my lips, invading the darkness with my sadness. I got up close to her ear. "I love you, I love you," I said softly.

She was tired; her dance classes and other athletic activities had worn her out. I fell asleep without realizing it. The cold woke me later; Carolina had uncovered me when she got up. It wasn't even light yet and she had gone to fulfill her mother's and Hosco's orders. "I'll be back at eleven," she said at five that morning.

"You won't be back," I said, sure of myself.

She didn't answer. I got up, sad and annoyed. I held her again, waiting for her eyes to tell me, "Yes, I'll be back." But her eyes lived in an unwritten poem, a star that had died thousands of years ago and that now gave off only a fictitious light. Her eyes told the truth: she hated me. I was doomed; I was a man who had been born for just two things: alcohol and jealousy.

I decided to go with her. She got dressed matter-of-factly; she had to obey her parents, and she had to destroy me, to shoot me, to abandon me.

It made me think of Mishima: "The measure of a woman's power is how much she makes the one who loves her suffer."

When we left there was just a bit of dawn showing; it was a delicate blue, like the one they use in the paintings of Christ sitting and weeping on the Mount of Olives. It was a senseless and disgusting dawn. After the orgasm and the penetration she was no more than a puppet living inside her own mediocrity. She knew she would never have a penis to penetrate me with and to show the world she could forget everything else. She envied me, and like all feminists, she put on her bracelets and went out to compete with the men who "for centuries have oppressed us poor women."

When we got out into the cold air, I felt that donkey's jawbone ready to strike. I had melted, I had led myself to my death using love as a weapon. I had been dragged down a dry and rocky river bed, tied to a horse. My face hurt, scratched by the cold and the death. I brought my hand to my face, I touched my nose, I felt the wounds I had gotten the last time I was drunk. I told her about it, hoping for mercy, hoping she wouldn't abandon me, but it only accelerated her sadism and quickened her steps toward her father's Ford.

Cannibal

She scornfully opened the car door for me. I got in, pissed as shit. "This is why you asked me to come?" I said.

"Don't start with me."

"I'm going to tell your parents that when I stick it up your ass you want to be my slave."

"You're crazy! Really, you should try to cure yourself, you are very sick."

"You used to like my craziness."

"You're a goddamned bore," she shot at me, like a South American soldier. "I know all your stories." She started the car. I asked her again to stay with me in the hotel. "No. I already told you I'm not going to just give everything up for you."

We drove away from a room that had witnessed our entire existence. The only place that would ever exist for us: room sixteen.

I lit what was left of my joint. I breathed in the smoke, trying to reach a calm, a wholeness, a catatonic state. Until on the way I finally exploded. "If you don't come with me, I don't want to see you again," I said.

"Well that sounds great," she said. "That's exactly what I want, for you to leave me alone. Go on, get out of here!"

I felt like crying for my father and I started weeping hysterically. I felt like a little girl. Like a coward. Sometimes I would look at her face, intent on driving fast so we'd get there sooner and she could toss me out of the car, to send me back to my apartment in Mexico City. All my dreams of the sea, of exotic fruits and salty perfumes had perished.

A monster had possessed her and he fed on my tears. If she could have, she would have tied me up and burned me with a cigarette on the same penis that gave her such pleasure. I imagined my semen dripping out from her rectum like an enema. I didn't even have the consolation of knowing that she would have something to remember me by.

From the moment I smelled her cadaver next to me I knew I would fall irretrievably into a nervous crisis, talking and talking with no chance of coming out of it until I fell exhausted on the keyboard, my eyes nailed to the letters, sighing when I saw the image of Carolina pass in front of me; bleeding, with a dirty pussy and an ass swollen by pleasure.

She sped the car up, as if chasing some phantom of happiness. I looked out the window at the streets where I used to hang out with my father. I cried for Carolina's death, for that of my brother who no longer appreciated me, for the death of my father, for the death of my ADN-infused spermatozoa that was now mixing with her feces, feces squashed by the tip of my billy club. "Fuck you!" I thought. "You betrayed me!"

We got to her house; I was still crying moronically. I should have done this a month ago when I was sitting with my father's ashes, but I was doing it now, as if death had arrived late for me, like a broken-down clock that made me cry at this moment, and now everyone and their ex-lovers, and my family, too, will send me to some institution, like I was a fucking crazy, a terrible twenty-eight-year-old freak of the eighties.

"Mike?" I thought to myself. "Is this the novel you wanted me to write?" Shit. "Get out of the car," she told me.

"I'm not getting out. I know you're going to leave me."

"I said get out."

"No," I said, still crying.

"Get out or you're really going to have problems."

I knew in a minute she'd call Hosco and he'd drag me out of the car.

I wanted to kill her, to strangle her, to kill myself. But it was no use, nothing was worth it, I wasn't really angry enough and I was too impotent. Wanting to make things right between us, I said, "Carolina! Just remember that whenever I stick it in your ass you get like this.

Can't you see you're hysterical? That you feel guilty? That you don't want to acknowledge your desires? I swear I'll never put it in your behind again, and never ever doggie style."

"Shut up, just stop the bullshit. Don't you understand how nervous you make me? Anyway, I have to go, I have to get ready for the community meeting."

"Fine, go make your little revolution, you and your fucking intellectual friends who have nothing left but to 'be in contact with the people.' Fucking clowns. Reading Marxist theory isn't what makes the revolution."

"You just say that because you're a goddamn spoiled rich kid."

"And you're a whore."

She began to scream. Crying and looking at her from within a cloud of water I couldn't ask her anything else but this. I remember she didn't say anything. Or maybe in her silence she was saying yes, that at least for a while she wouldn't use the garters and the underpants we liked so much.

Before I had even turned the corner I took out a cigarette, pretending to be like a leading man from the movies who bids farewell to his love for the last time. I was crying so hard I lit the wrong end. I threw the cigarette down and spat on the ground. Then I took out another and lit it, but I was still crying and it tasted disgusting, and I threw that one down too. The neighbors saw a tall man with a beard crying and standing at a woman's door, instead of crying when his father died. I arrived at the same conclusion as they did: I was schizophrenic. I kept on walking. "They should all go fuck their mothers," I said to myself.

Out With It!

"Todaaaay I wannnt to taaaste my own paaaain, I ask for nooooo compaaassion or pity ...," José José was singing.

His voice came from a store that sold jewelry and accessories, the kind Carolina wore. "Right now," I was thinking, "the only thing I want is a toke, a Valium, and to crawl into the bed where my father used to sleep." I started off in the direction of my house, feeling really pissed. I saw my brother just coming home, drunk. "You were such a wimp with her," he says to me. "You're drinking over a woman, and you're trying to give me advice?" I think, and then I remember my mother, almost down on her knees on the telephone begging me NOT TO FIGHT WITH MY BROTHER.

So I decided not to make things worse, but just to grab my things: the bathing suit I was supposedly going to use with Carolina tomorrow at the beach, the cassettes that Carolina and I would supposedly be listening to, the condoms that I was supposedly going to use with Carolina, and a piece of shit book by Jaime Sabines that I was going to read with the asshole Carolina.

I leave the house like a shot and head for my Caribe, put on my anti-plutonium glasses and set out en route to the asphalt jungle.

Mexico City, Distrito Federal! Wait for me; I'm coming back—to your traffic, to feel the delicacies of an exhaust pipe in my upturned nose. Distrito Federal, hold on, I'm coming in my Caribe, I'll strip myself of my class so I can make the revolution. What else is left for me?

Distrito Federal, I love you, earthquakes and all; I want to die under a building, in the mud and the rats, and not in this shitty joke of a fucking town.

I was incredibly pissed off, I was speeding all the way, I didn't give a shit if I crashed. I was returning with three cadavers: my father, my woman, and my brother. I felt like I was missing a leg, an arm, and an eye. Like I was coming back from the war.

But no, I shouldn't think that way, I should do what my friend Rogelio says: "Think about poor people; your worries are petit-bourgeois." It's true; I should pay more attention to Rogelio. "I'm a bourgeois, I'm a bourgeois, I shouldn't worry about stupid things." Sniff, sniff.

"I'm prisoner of the webs of a poem," José José was singing at full volume. I had a walkman, the kind they sell at the Tepito market. My bass vibrated at a thousand per hour. I felt like Jalapa was coming after me. I knew if I looked in the rear view mirror I'd turn to stone. I passed mountains, sidewalks, poor people, fucked-up people, broken-down cars, and a dead dog on the middle of the highway; I got it out from the wheels but its thorax was still smashed against the car. I went faster, turned up the walkman, picked up a half a joint I had in the ashtray and lit it as best I could. I took two huge tokes, held in the smoke, and as José José was singing I shouted, "Long live pot!"

Luckily I had two or three connections, enough to keep me in dope while I write my immortal novel. They had gotten me some 'redhead', a magnificent marijuana where the pistils of the flowers look like the pubic hair of a redhead vagrant wandering the streets of New York.

I couldn't stop thinking about my misery and the trip seemed all too short. My mind had activated a defense mechanism to avoid all thoughts of highways, to make me think it was a nightmare, a mistake of censored dreams. I was at war with the world once more.

On the way I was thinking about a professor of psychoanalysis who told me that novels tended to drift off course, while a short story was tenser.

That's why I feel my life is like a short story.

One time, when I was at Ocho y Medio, sober, a guy asked me what drug I used to speed myself up so much. I told him I wasn't on anything, but since then I realized that my Eros and my Thanatos were galloping toward hell, that any minute I would just topple over.

I slowed the car down on a hill with steep turns; I had no other choice but to keep on living, and that was the worst! But if I killed myself someone else would get to screw her. Holy shit! There was nothing I could do. Now everything would be different: we would never be the same to each other.

At the moment when you think, “I wish she were here with me,” everything was fucked and worth shit.

I put on a cassette of Javier Solis. “Which lips are clooosing your eyyyyeees, your eyyyyyes that I closed with my kisses, the mornings are like daggers, prison won’t kill me, but your cursed love will.” That’s the way to go, Javier! Again: “Which lips are clooooosing your eyyyeees ….”

Miserable, despicable whore, that piece of shit. I wanted to go back just to whip her butt. But I was the one who was a fool. I had imagined myself with a house by now, with blond children in the backyard tossing a ball around. I had wanted to have a happy family! Sniff, sniff.

I part the sea of smog that covers my immense city and I think sadly: Oh my beautiful Mexico, I will never leave you.

Return to Nothing

At the first stoplight I realized I was in Mexico City. Everyone waiting for the light to change. One, two, three, four minutes. We'd speed up just to stop again two hundred yards later at the next light: one, two, three, four, five minutes. We move forward three hundred yards and stop at another light one, two, three, four, sometimes ten minutes.

That's it! Sociology had given me the answer. Carolina had run away from Mexico City to avoid losing herself among millions of individuals and filling her blood with lead; she'd rather be the head of a mouse than the tail of a lion. Nietzsche said: "You want to be a hero? Turn snakes into dragons!" That's the good thing about Mexico City. From the minute you wake up you have a thin film of shit covering your head, and you sleep in the middle of thousands of gas tanks, and any day you could wake up roasted; you face death daily. These were not philosophical deliberations, rather it was a way to relax my body, giving myself little cultural maxims to help me pass the time between stoplights.

Everyone moving slowly, united by the radio that keeps pumping out its shit. I remember I agreed to give Mike the novel in twenty-eight days, the time it takes for a woman's, or two women's, dead ovaries to complete their cycle. Could be Carolina's and Pamela's, or Eloisa's, but I can't write about her because her father's a politician and he could send someone to rough me up.

It's difficult to describe twenty-eight days, to be between one abortion and the next. Or even worse, to be like I've said thousands of times in periods of madness: merely surviving. Life between ejaculations is a period of stagnation; only the great gusts of an ejaculation onto the uteral neck of a woman can prove interesting. Watching television, sitting quietly in front of a baseball game: these things never happen to me. My libido pulls me by the dick at least three times a week; I come into the darkness of my own eyelids, and I die. I look through my address book while I'm stopped at a light, anxiously searching from A to Z for the telephone number of some girl whose pants I can get into without having to do too much for it.

My God! And if while I'm thinking this Carolina already has some other guy between her legs?

A tortuous thought: a fortuneteller introduces himself to me. "Within the hour Carolina will screw a ballet dancer who everyone thought was a fag but turned out to be straight," he tells me, "and you must drive four hours in order to stop her by kicking down the door." What a horrible nightmare, I think, pained. Maybe she's already done it. Shit. Gulp.

A pack of monsters with green eyes gnaws at my chest, jealousy imprisons my scrotal sac and shrivels it up, traveling languidly from belly to throat; put into words this would be called fear, and anger. To top it off, I imagine her with someone who talks about other things besides jealousy and alcohol.

A policeman starts arguing with a taxi driver. At my left a bus stops and burps exhaust right into my window. I think about the men who kill themselves in North American garages by stopping up the doors and suffocating from the smoke. I pray to Jesus that the police and the taxi driver stop fighting. The smoke settles in my car, my fault for not having closed the window before; finally the argument ends and we advance some five hundred yards. Damn, my girlfriend's fucking someone else and everyone's snailing along here. Bastards. A guy comes up to squirt some soap on my windshield; he starts washing it and I put my hand into my pocket, looking for a hundred peso piece. I can't find it, he finishes cleaning and a Galaxy bumps into me from behind; they're cops. The guy doesn't get his money, the cops keep moving forward, almost pushing me, an out-of-tune Opal goes by spurting out blue smoke, I light a cigarette, I breathe in the smoke, and I feel the pleasure of self-destruction. I feel content to be back in Mexico City.

There's just one small problem: I'm not happy, because I'm not sure how long Carolina can go without a dick.

I know I'm going to end up buying *When Lovers Part* by Igor Caruso; I remember buying it when I broke up with Pamela, but I think I lent it to Leopardo when he broke up with Martha.

At this time of day I should be on the beach with Carolina, enjoying the view, watching the seagulls, but no, no, fuck everything, and now, what the goddamn hell am I going to do in Mexico City? What can I do? I don't need to work. I would give myself a goal, oh, I know: to find two joints every day. This is a great plan in life, locking myself away to read *Remembrance of Things Past*, slowly and carefully, to be next to Marcel Proust for seven volumes, next to a window waiting for Carolina, believing she'll get there before I accept the end of our relationship as the only reason for the wait. To lock myself up with the seven volumes and assure myself that when I finish reading them I would be at least fifty years old and maybe Carolina would be dead or would have a grandson, who would have never heard about the poor idiot stopped by two hundred stoplights before getting home where I will collapse into solitude, suffering the destruction that I myself provoked, finding refuge in a black hole, cursed, badly written, perverse, where now for sure some intellectual is fucking Carolina doggie style.

Yeah, that's it, and Pamela too, that one's for sure; now the young professional must have her really hot, with her legs over his shoulders, pulling down on her knees, entrapping all feeling, like an arrow that stretches across a bow, a pussy that receives the thrust of my own death.

But my friend Rogelio says I shouldn't be so dramatic. Sure, I shouldn't be so dramatic, I shouldn't be so dramatic. Fucking hell. Sniff, sniff.

Drunk with jealousy, tobacco and grass, I come to my building. I take my suitcase out of the car so I can forget that a moron went on a trip in search of love. Shit. I press the button for the elevator; the tenuous signal indicates that it has started to move; it takes twenty-five seconds to come down. It's on the sixth floor, and since this is my floor, I know exactly how long it takes. What if the elevator was on the sixth floor because Carolina, regretful, had come to save a poet from his own destruction?

I must be dreaming. I think about my father and I start to snivel, the elevator opens itself up to me like a vertical tomb, I get to my floor in twenty-two seconds, it seems strange that it takes longer to go down than to go up, I get out, I'm six floors above the earth. I go towards my door, I turn the key in the lock and in front of me appears an empty space where an abandoned man will soon be rotting. To find myself in the same place I had left the day before, at the same time, but now without my woman, gives me an existential swoon. I rush to the bureau, I take out two Ativáns and I swallow them, waiting to feel sleepy, thinking about how to stop thinking that I am rotting away from impotence. How does one stop thinking? I walk in circles around the apartment. I look at the spines of a shitload of books of writers who have already written their immortal novels. I feel a profound envy.

How long will Carolina last until she starts to look at men?

I throw myself onto the bed, and to make it worse, since I couldn't do it last time with her, I feel horny. I rub up against the mattress; I don't really want to masturbate, but when I come I'll think about Carolina and I'll feel a bitter and delirious orgasm. I'd rather wait for the chemical to begin to act on my brain and dull my senses until I fall flat on my face into a heavy sleep, surrounded by ferocious women who chew on my testicles while a eunuch with an impossible hard-on tells them better jokes than mine. Shit. And I fall asleep.

Prisoner of Love

I wake up at nine p.m. Dressed, under an itchy bedspread. I prefer not to get undressed and then have to think: I am naked and alone.

That's why, when I felt the rough bedspread on the back of my fingers, flaking off my cuticles, it gave me a chill, and my first thought was: my woman and I are finished. And I kept feeling sorry for myself until I starting saying that my misery was for the death of my father and nothing else, but my unconscious played tricks on me and manifested itself on the rotted peach skin of Carolina, her hollow and unspeakable voice mortifying my memory.

It was completely dark; at times the headlights of a car reflecting on stone walls and windows came in through the curtains. "That's something, at least I'm not blind!" I thought.

I looked for the switch on the lamp cord, groping for it, squeezing carefully. But my hand went to the wrong end: toward the plug. With my arm twisted, in pain from the stupid maneuvering, I walk my fingers along the cord as if my hand were an animal that wanted to eat it. But when I find the switch the light still doesn't go on; I remember the electricity has been turned off, they shut it off exactly yesterday, and that was my pretext for going to see Carolina.

I remember I had said at the time, "Alone, abandoned, no electricity, no! I'm going to Jalapa to see the woman who loves me."

And now it's darker—yesterday I left during the day—I'm even more abandoned, in an abortive solitude. I have been expelled from the womb of Carolina by a poison.

My jeans smell of the highway and burnt oil. I feel ridiculous, tremulous and dejected. I didn't know what 'tremulous' meant, but that's how I felt. I remembered that I had to be a great writer and I told myself that no one knows who Balzac's women were, or Proust's, or those of any other great men who, in my solitude, I could compare myself to.

I believed in literature like a boy who's afraid of a well and then sees the bucket that will save him from the bottom.

I felt ridiculous lying there under the bedspread, thinking about it being nine at night. This was the worst part; the whole world would be going to sleep, throwing me even deeper into my own solitude, as if a whirlpool of blood fell through my ventricles and veins, like someone swimming around inside his own heart. I remembered Carolina's body, I remembered her breasts and her downy hair. She had killed me.

I instinctively look for my lighter in the left pocket of my shirt, stick in my hand, and when I press the pack of cigarettes against my chest I know why I had dreamed of being tortured; I had fallen asleep on the lighter, smashing it against my nipple. I light it and get up to look for a candle in the desk drawer. On the way my bare foot trips against the leg of the table the TV sits on and I feel a profound pain in my toes, in my bones. I sit down on the bed and the light from the lighter goes out. I rub my toes as if enjoying the pain and that way, sitting with my head between my hands, I pass my hands over my eyes without knowing if they're open or closed, as if by crying I had left them insensible to touch. My lost gaze sees shapes in the darkness. I ask myself what good it would do to get up to light the candle. I wasn't hungry, or thirsty, all I wanted was a cigarette and that was in my pocket.

Lighting a candle would have driven me to search for something beyond my boredom, to pick up the telephone and call Carolina. To beg her once again. To ask her to forgive me, to tell her that she was right, that I was the bad one, and was out of line. That's why it was better to be in the dark; I was no longer in a hurry for anything, I no longer had to pace in despair, waiting for her in a brightly lit room.

Now she would never be back and I had all the time in the world to lie there, remembering, lighting a Camel, trying to feel important. But suddenly a horrible thought came to my mind: what would happen after I finished this cigarette? I shouldn't light another. I had to sleep with my mouth almost half-open from the putrefaction of so much tobacco and marijuana. I wouldn't light a cigarette after this one, no, I would just lie there quietly, like those dogs who "look like they're thinking".

That's why I smoked the cigarette slowly; I liked seeing the room light up with every drag. I remembered some Freudians who said that cigarettes represent the presence of an idealized but destructive mother.

The truth is I didn't know what was going to happen after this cigarette. I had barely begun to think about it and I already felt the taste of tar at the end; the cigarette would soon be smoked up, I'd inevitably come to the filter, or burn my fingers even before I got there, and I'd have to say: It's finished! Now what?

I put it out and sadly took off my shirt; I was a little warm, but only a little; I really just wanted to touch my bare arms and shoulders and pretend they were Carolina's.

But when my shoulders felt the caresses and the misdirected sensuality of my hands, I became imprisoned by terror. I wasn't using my palms completely like when they rest over my loved one, no, I was alone, masturbating unerotically, waiting for her sighs, not my hacking cough that every now and then cut the room in two. This choking and cacophonous cough at times made me want to vomit; I had to control myself so I wouldn't fall into convulsions. My lungs were a black hole that I was falling deeper and deeper into: my own insides, cancerous at twenty-eight years old.

I wanted to know what Carolina was doing right then. To know her thoughts, to think the same things she was thinking, like two synchronized watches; but who was better or worse off? She or I?

Maybe she wasn't even thinking about me; maybe she was making salsa in her parents' house, watching the blender so it didn't splatter over everything, or maybe thinking about some new boy she met and how great it was that she'd met him at that time and not some other.

When my father died even she couldn't keep me sane; how lucky for her to meet someone with electroencephalographic waves just like hers. Someone normal, someone with her tastes, or simply someone new, so when he flattered her on her clothes she could bask in the attentions of a new man and not of an alcoholic like me who got bored with his woman after two years.

"She's probably asleep," I thought. But it was a Friday night at nine o'clock; she could be lying awake, feeling drained and sad.

Maybe she's getting ready to go out to La Atasca again. My testicles feel like they've been swept out by a street cleaner. I look for the lighter, get up for a candle, light it, and that's when, in a sudden burst of ardor, I dial her number. Her mother answers and says that Carolina went with her father to some village and she didn't know when they'd be back.

This makes me feel even worse. I feel sad that I called her; when she finds out she'll say, "If he's suffering, then why do I have to?"

It wasn't only the jealousy I felt for Hosco, that really wasn't so much. It bothered me more to think, "What a bitch! If I had stayed there, she'd be gone anyway, off on a honeymoon with her father." And that was what hurt me most, knowing that the trick had already been planned. She would have said to me, all sweet and entreating: "You'd better go now, I have to go with my father." When a woman wants to hurt you it doesn't matter that years go by between the desire and act.

When she was a little girl she lived a fairy-tale life, with someone always nearby to play with her and celebrate her charming ways. Now I had vacated my own body and was much more morbid than usual, and this frightened her because she was sick of dealing with someone who didn't give her the thing women want most: someone to tell them complete bullshit.

I was still sitting on the edge of the bed; my feet stank from so much highway and I felt filthy. The lit candle sketched my anxious shadow against the wall.

We had lived here together for two years and everything reminded me of her. I was tired of looking at the same thing and I decided to go out. I pulled myself together, putting on the same sweaty shirt. I didn't want to go out looking for a girl. I was like an infant, waking up every three hours to cry. That's what they say about people who have been abandoned: they go back to infancy. In order to break up you need hamburgers and aquavit: handle it, and know your life is shit.

I was going out to get fucked up, and speaking of getting fucked, there was some really loud music coming from the second floor. I left my apartment, got in the elevator, and pushed the button for floor number two. I wanted to go spy on the bash. The elevator stopped at two; you could hear eighties music playing, it sounded like Phil Collins. But you could hear even better what was going on behind it: "It's my turn now! Suck me!" three voices were saying like hungry little birds.

"No, you already fucked her," someone said in a drunken voice.

"So what, I can get it up as many times as I fuckin' please!"

"Shut up you bastards, or I'll shut you up myself," a third alcoholic voice said.

"Hey, give me a chance to get comfortable," the girl was saying.

"What if Carolina's doing the same thing in Jalapa?" my sick mind thought, feverishly paranoid. Aaaargh!—went my subconscious.

I got into the elevator, trying to forget what I had just heard.

I opened the front door of the building and the cold air hit me in the face. It wasn't nine o'clock anymore, it was eleven, and the world was closed to a lonely man. I walked to the Sanborn's on the corner. There were guards making sure no one stole any books, the restaurant was filled with bums and Jews, and three drunks were slumped over the bar, paying with the credit card of an ex-Alcoholics Anonymous who had fallen off the wagon.

I went to the book and magazine section. I felt dizzy and almost vomited when I saw the competition I was facing. Bukowski says the worst thing that can happen to a writer is to meet another writer. I saw so many books, I wanted to piss on them all, to take mine out and say to everyone: Here I am, you bastards, I need you to make me famous so Carolina will come back to me!

I looked at the covers without seeing them, my mind was possessed. But something made me come out of my stupor: a gun magazine. It was a gringo magazine that sold everything, even little golf carts used for killing Vietnamese. They also sold tee-shirts with Gadhafi in a telescope sight. One thing the gringos aren't is boring; they also had a section dedicated to training Marxist-killers. A tough looking guy, a Rambo type, was hanging off on a cliff, holding a high-power weapon. The price was listed below.

And now how was I going to maintain my war against the world without my true love waiting for me somewhere? I remembered that Agent 007 never lacked women; he always had his piece of ass waiting for him on some Adriatic island, while a goddamn skinny blonde won't even wait for me in a hotel room in Jalapa.

I felt bad; since I was little I had always wanted to be a playboy and instead I was turning into a vulgar imbecile.

I promised myself that at thirty I would stop thinking of women as the essential part of my life, that by magic I would stop needing a girl to accompany me to museums, stop needing to be a little married intellectual who educates his children on Freud, Marx and Melanie Klein, at the same time fighting all day with his woman because one of them thinks the revolution should start in the city and not in the hills, or that Leon Davidovich Trotsky is more right-on than Gramsci, or other absurd pseudo-war-of-the-classes conversations that would pull our guts out from below the balls, the ovaries and the shoes, and leave us exhausted, with no sexual desire left, because we would only see each other to screw. The relationship would have died long before, just like Carolina has died and just like, as Nietzsche says, "God is dead; his pity for men is what killed him."

I lean out the door; there was a flower vender who looked like she was dying of hunger leaning against a window of Sanborn's.

It's true, that's why Carolina left me; I had promised during some drunken binge to be her Che, and I never did it.

I talked to her about feminism like an expert. I felt real liberal; afterwards we would screw and screw and screw and that rid us of our revolutionary anxieties; instead we would start to say that the poor are the ones who have to make the revolution, that we were acting only out of guilt and that, knowing this, we shouldn't do it.

Finding myself without a woman killed the revolution for me, and all the doors of the Marxist academies were shut in my face; besides, my other book had shut me out of all the fascist institutions, like the Department of Letters at UNAM, the National Autonomous University of Mexico.

I started walking along Insurgentes. As much as I tried to feel like Robert Redford, I couldn't do it; I realized how pitiful my little stupid being and my little stupid sadness was.

In those days the book *The Unbearable Lightness of Being* was all the rage. I didn't have it, I hadn't read it. Like many intellectual couples who spoke of him I thought it might help me.

As I was thinking one moronic thing after another, I remembered the day I went to the oral exams of a girl who was studying in the Literature Department at UNAM. Her thesis was on 'Lyricism in Rock and Roll.' The room was, as always, filled with the parents and friends of the accused. The jury was composed of three people: two in ties and a woman we called 'Miss Righter'.

The guys in ties barely moved; they were sitting straight up in their chairs as if they were about to fart. "As for Donovan," the one on the right said, straightening his tie, "I don't believe Donovan is really a good poet."

I remember I was there with Marta. Marta had wanted to study literature but some invisible force had her removed from the department. That's right. I remember she told me that one of the men on the panel was named Cristóbal; he had been a 'friend' of hers, until one day he said to her, "You don't belong in English literature; where you really belong is with a psychiatrist."

Marta was in English literature because her father had always asked her to "do something with your life," but she didn't care about anything except rock. "All they do here is teach you how to count syllables," she told me.

During the exam Miss Righter interrogated the examinee in English. Everyone was so excited to hear Gringo spoken. I have never understood why we learn English and not Chinese since there are more Chinese people than people who speak English. I'm a jerk.

They were playing it to the hilt. I understood about half of it. My English is whatever I managed to remember from the books in school. Just the essentials, enough to be able to work as a boatman in Acapulco.

Even Cristóbal said something to the professor IN ENGLISH. Can you imagine? Isn't it so touching you just want to cry? Cristóbal speaks English, too. Ooooh, God of Letters, please forgive my ignorance in not knowing your name, but as you know: YOU MUST SPEAK ENGLISH IN ORDER TO BE A POET. What an ass I am!

One day a psychoanalyst friend of mine gave me his interpretation of why I resent gringos so much. He said it was because as a boy I hadn't learned to speak English. But I really must be an imbecile, one must hear the euphony of the gringos, I must just be envious.

It doesn't matter if you really feel one of Poe's poems as he felt it, the important thing is to recite it IN ENGLISH. Ahhh, and if you put a footnote in a book it has to be IN ENGLISH. And be careful: if you put the translation below, it'll look tacky.

I gave one of my books to Cristóbal and his colleagues. They treated me well, I treated them well. A phrase from Nietzsche came to mind: "If you want someone to help you, flatter them first." (A cynical piece of advice ....)

There was no reason to fight about it, because without weapons we wouldn't have gotten anywhere, and they would end up thinking the same way and so would I.

It would have been better if they'd had a bit of psychopathy and if I had some of their obsessive neurosis. We would then balance out and that way we could have been either guerillas or fascists.

My body arrived at the corner. Now and then a drunk sped by in a car; I remembered the events of the second floor in my building, and I felt alone. I turned halfway around and I thought, "What is Carolina looking at right now?"

On the way back I saw three families of *marías*, our own version of the homeless, a drunk with his nose plastered against the sidewalk, and about twenty rats.

I went back up to my apartment and stopped again on the second floor. The guys were still raising a ruckus and I could hear them saying to the girl, "How do you want to do it? How do you like it? Huh?"

"Hey, give me a chance to get comfortable."

Then one of them shouted in a shrill voice, "I want it doggie style, let's do it doggie style! Don't you like it that way, babe? Come on, let's do doggie style."

I clutched at my chest; I was excluded from the party. I would have to go up to my apartment and go to sleep, while I fantasized that on the second floor they were screwing some Carolina who had probably just broken up with her boyfriend because he was too jealous. Sigh.

Riiiiiing!

"He who loves cannot think, he gives it aaalll, he gives it aaalll, he who desires tries to forget and neeeever cry, neeever cry," José José sang into my tape from inside my tape player.

Carolina's message was still on my answering machine. "My love, where are you, when are you corning?" was still there, hypocritical and absurd. It was like listening to the beginning of a story I already knew.

She had left me this message the day before I left to look for her, and there it was, like a death sentence. I listened to it five times, looking for traces of cynicism in her voice. But there weren't any, she was totally trapped in the animus, the Jungians would say, trapped by the devil who invades in the form of cynicism.

The telephone rings and I answer it; it's Angel. I tell him about it. "You're just pissed because you wanted to hit her and you couldn't," he says. We hang up.

It rings again and it's Rogelio. I tell him about it. "I'll call you back later. You know how women are," he says. We hang up.

It rings again and it's Mike. I tell him about it. "At least it lasted for a while; in the nineties all they're going to do is screw us and then dump us. Besides, you can't cure her! She's always going to prefer her father," he says. We hang up.

It rings again; it's Maggi. I tell her about it. "When I broke up with my boyfriend I felt really great; I could do whatever I wanted," she says. We hang up.

It rings again; it's Ernesto. I tell him about it. "Oh, please. Are you really surprised? You knew it was coming," he says. We hang up.

It rings again; it's Martha. I tell her about it. "What are you complaining about you bastard, you were always so goddamn macho with her," she says. We hang up.

"What was before will never be agaaiin, you will never look for me, I have nooothing to giiive youuuu, I'm tired of the birdseed you gave me, go fly off to another sky and keep your cage door open; perhaps another sparrow will fall, but be sure to give it something to drink," José José is singing.

Pamela

It was strange; I barely thought about Pamela. When I broke up with her I felt just like I did now in my new failure. I even went to go chain myself, drunk, to her front door to get her to go out with me. Angel and some other friends came to save me.

Thinking about Pamela was disastrous for one simple reason: she was married. And she told me she made love with her husband every morning. And Carolina? Was she going to do it at night?

Pamela was the response to the question of what was waiting for me with the next one and the next and the next. Hiding behind masks until our bodies fall to pieces. Shit. I would never have a happy family. And ever since I was young I've believed the ads on TV. Christ.

Pamela had found what she wanted, someone to buy her two VCRs and a nice car, company, somewhere she could be a mother for a while and, above all, a man who GOES TO WORK EVERY DAY and isn't a sloth like me, me who only wanted—and still wants—to be stuck like a sucker fish on a woman's breast.

Thinking about Pamela led me to an even bigger headache, which was Carolina. I felt sick, knowing that she would get married and that her husband would be the one screwing her.

I went towards the mirror, the one always present in immortal novels, the mirror I wanted to stick my hand in so I could pluck my eyes out and squash them onto the paper.

Only a torrential, bloody cry could keep me sane in my godawful solitude. "Your problem is, you never had to work for a living," my father would say.

Pamela called me to say that I should be happy that we were going to see each other again. Now she was back, full of holes from screwing so much in Cancún.

I should be grateful for the favor; she came down from Mt. Olympus, from her thousands of jobs, to take the trouble to call me just to say,

"Remember how much we loved each other? Oh, I gotta go, I have to go make dinner for my husband."

That's why I should be happy and not denounce life. I had to get used to the idea that when we were old we would all be friends and that we would never screw again. Tender images that I found stupid and horrifying.

In the eighties women were happy because they wanted it all and they just about had it. Since they could eventually get their fangs into anyone they chose, they didn't have any problems, everything was at their disposal; it was just a matter of grabbing one on the street and raising their skirts, showing pubic hair that smelled like jism.

And we men were like dogs. The only girls who didn't have boyfriends were the ones still waiting for their white knight, or the ones who demanded love and intimacy before they'd fuck. But their pussy was there, waiting, desperate; a universal language, the pussy; the Esperanto of uneducated women and the desperation of my life. We had all been pushed out through a pussy and those who came by Caesarian were just as selfish. Everything was fucked up.

Maybe Carolina is doing it doggie style as I write this, or maybe I'm just projecting my filthy, drooling instincts on to her and it's me who wants to be doing it doggie style, be to be pierced by my father-in-law, my father, Christ, and the devil. I was dying, and thinking about Pamela didn't help; on the contrary, it made me sadder and flung me even closer to solitude. So much that I felt like 'Prometheus Bound', as well as somewhat of a jackass.

Meeee, the playboy, who the twenty-year old girls called a love terrorist.

Could it be because of my body? I had a potbelly, sure, but I only let it go because Pamela and Carolina always said to me, "I love your belly." Thanks a lot, girls.

And now, potbellied and blond, I felt like a skinny dog from the country. Potbellied and dirty. At least I wasn't drunk; it would be worse to be hung-over in this condition.

I remember one month before my father died my cousin told me a story about him in front of everyone. My mother and I were horrified and left the room.

It seems that when he married my mother, my cousins were still little kids and my father took them to watch how they killed pigs for barbecue.

Really it didn't bother me to speak badly about my father after his death. This is a sign of my schizophrenia, of my abnormality. Although there are some who are bothered by it, but then end up saying: Papa always beat me, Mama never hugged me.

Even though my father didn't beat me and my mother did hug me, I believe that what interfered between us was language. Language always so different from action, like a song in a foreign tongue that you think says something different from what it really says.

I've hated children since I was one myself. I'd get really mad when I was forced to go out to play basketball or soccer, and I'd get pissed off when they all told me how strange I was because I wanted to be around adults. I loved imitating them. Ever since I was five my mother would say to me, "Come on, honey, imitate your uncle Rafael." And I would do it, and everyone would laugh. And now I'm grown up and I realize that being an adult is no great shakes.

Before he died, my father listened to the poems from my book and paid for me to publish an edition of ten thousand copies. One year earlier, when he was still healthy, he wanted to disown me and even told me to change my last name.

I get up to roll a joint.

All the potheads I know like to write when they're stoned. People act like cats when they're high. Animals are real stoners, caught in that state where you just hang around like a hanger and think about absolutely nothing. It would be interesting to be reincarnated as an animal and not need pot to get to that state of mind. Living without bad trips, just looking for food, not having to write like Thomas

Mann or Proust so people will love us.

What an idea! I want to be an animal poet.

An animal poet who writes anti-novels: everything has already been said, said the wandering bird who carries my father's ashes. Everything has been said and I collapse into sleep.

Ain't Too Proud to Beg

The next morning I feel a fetid pain when I remember I'm 'divorced'; I decide to send Carolina some letters along the lines of, "Dear Carolina, I'm sorry I forgot to tell you about my gonorrhea ...." Something ridiculous like that. Anyway, I found a photo of us hugging. I was going to send her at least three copies of it in case someone found one of them and threw it away.

Then it was Pamela on the phone. "Hi," she says.

"Hi," I answer.

"I just called to tell you I'll call you later. Bye."

"Bye."

Pamela always called me to say the same thing. She's phallocentric just like Carolina, and always competing for men. Her husband had never disappointed her in any way and now she wants a divorce because she can't talk to him. She likes to talk to me and she doesn't have time to do it.

I like the photo of me and Carolina hugging, but to everyone else it looks like the corniest thing imaginable. The thought bothers me and I stop on the street. "They're going to laugh at me at the copy place. Such a big, tall, goofy baby," I say to myself.

I go to a shop where they don't know me. That way I can make something up. When I get there I give the photo to the woman. I hand it to her face down so she won't see it, and then something worse happens: she realizes what I'm planning to do with it! She turns it over, curious as a cat. "See, I used to work with this girl on a photonovella and these are some tests we did," I say to her. I think she believed me. And when I had left, I realized I didn't owe her any explanation. But I still imagined everyone saying, "Jeeeeesus, how embarrassing! Aren't you embarrassed to be so pitiful? Get up off your knees, you goddamn wimp fag. There you go again, begging like a dog."

But I wanted Carolina to have a copy of the picture and at least to think about when we took it.

I was on my way home when two women passed in front of me.

You

One had eyes like hooks, piercing me. The other looked at me and then lowered her eyes to the ground. They went in a small door. I thought about going home to write the letters to Carolina, but my life-loving mind and my abandoned pecker dragged me after them.

In the entrance I saw a staircase covered in gray carpeting that led to a beauty salon, or at least that's what I thought it was. Inside you could hear The Police on the radio.

Two policemen were going up the stairs, looking for hookers. Turns out the place was a brothel.

It wasn't only a brothel for women, they also had men. The decoration didn't matter, just say there were two long couches where the hookers sit to read comic books.

There was a fat one who the girls called Doughboy; she had cellulite on top of her cellulite, they said.

Her legs were so fat she couldn't close them all the way and you could see some hairs that looked like black stripes on a prison wall. The important thing is that's where I met Yoli. She was a prostitute with a Cuban ass; big, that is, and hard. Spectacular breasts and a nose that made me think of a statue. "Hi. Look, I'm a magician," I said, making a cigarette disappear. I gave her all my credentials, thinking women like that kind of stuff.

"Wow, that's cool!"

Then we talked about poetry. I was getting horny, surrounded by so much flesh, legs and low necklines, and I felt the emotion well up in my throat. I asked her if she wanted to go with me to get something to eat; she said yes. On the way for some hamburgers I decided to take her to my apartment. When we got there I lit a joint and we started talking.

I thought she could be my Ylajali. But Ylajali should be a virgin, that's how the unknown woman of my dreams must be. But then again, why should Ylajali be a virgin?

Pamela had told me on the telephone that "everyone screws now" and I should just accept it and forget the demands of my father, my mother, and all the dirty words hidden deep in my spirit.

I felt bad when I started to touch her; a prostitute, so they say, fucks whether she likes it or not. But even so I didn't give up on the idea.

She could have some disease, AIDS, or whatever, but my skin was so lonely I didn't care about the risk; she even said to me, guessing my thoughts, "There are more diseases among the girls they call 'decent' than we have." She charged twelve thousand pesos, so I guessed she wouldn't have many customers like me, at least that's what I wanted to think.

The fact that she didn't charge me and that she dared to stick my penis all the way to the back of her throat touched me, it made me think she loved me, that she had never loved anyone like she loved me, that she had never possessed a man like she possessed me. That my dick was the only one that had ever existed on earth.

Then she got on top of me. She had breasts four times bigger than Carolina's and three times bigger than Pamela's. The minute I put it in her I knew I was going to come. "I'm not going to last very long in here, this is just too hot for me," I said to her. She got off me and as she sucked me my thoughts were filled with love: "Why does she suck me so passionately when her clitoris isn't anywhere near her mouth?" Maybe it's because I told her I was the only man on earth, and the Vivaldi on the stereo seemed to verify it. "I'm an idiot," I thought.

Later she pulled me into her again and I came, thinking about Carolina, about Pamela, about Yoli's ex-husband who had left her out of jealousy; I thought about AIDS, about my good luck, about how I wanted to die right then. After I came I said, "And we were only going for hamburgers."

"And you came back with a real meal," she said, grinning.

She went in to take a shower, and I joined her in a gesture of affection; even though she wasn't Ylajali she did have something mysterious about her.

The mystery of being a prostitute.

I didn't want to fall into stupid romanticizing; after we exchanged telephone numbers I gave her an invitation that Mike had designed for Ocho y Medio; it showed a man in an "I want to fuck you" pose, standing in front of a woman in an "I don't want you to, but do it" pose. The card said: "Romantic Indiscretions." A card that she would end up leaving next to my telephone; she never called me.

I remember that when I closed the door I felt like I should be happy, that I was obliged to feel happy, happy that I had been able to turn over my hourglass and go on.

In that instant the telephone rang; it was Pamela. "Hi."

"Hi," I said. I told her I was really depressed by what had happened with Carolina. I told her about Yoli, about my sadness. "I've learned to have a vaginal orgasm with my husband," she said.

"He must really be a stud in bed."

"No. It's because I've matured psychologically."

"So you'd be able to have a vaginal orgasm with me?"

"With you and with anyone."

She talked about how bad her marriage was with her engineer and asked me to help her deal with the pain. We made a plan to meet at five o'clock in front of the giant clock made of flowers in Hundido Park.

I got there at exactly five o'clock. I waited five, then ten, then twenty minutes. Finally a figure in white, with three bracelets on one wrist, two on the other, rings—one was a diamond—and a loving expression in its dark brown, almost black eyes, came washing over me. We both shifted slightly and I turned to look at the ground as if I had only just barely seen her and wasn't sure it was her. I did it out of embarrassment for the other people who were there—it was a bunch of teenagers shoving each other around, feigning that happiness that exists but isn't yet a part in their sexual personae. Oh, how literary I was feeling!

When she reached me I didn't hold out my hand, we didn't even say hello to each other. We started walking as if we had a predetermined destination, a place that would hide us even from ourselves. After we had gone about fifteen steps I told her I didn't have much time, that I had to go to my analyst. "God, you're so dependent on your therapy," she said.

"It's because I believe in him more than in you, besides, he won't abandon me; I have enough money to keep paying him."

"I am going to help you."

"Will you come with me?"

"No."

"That's okay. So anyway, how are you? What have you been doing?"

"Nothing much. I think my husband and I are going to get a separation and I'm going to marry someone else."

"Do you have someone in mind?"

"No."

"So why do you want to get married again?"

"I don't know, I just do."

We stayed quiet for a minute and then she said, "You are my true love. I've never loved anyone like I loved you."

"Oh yeah?"

"Well, I've been in love nine times, but you were the hardest one to break up with."

"Hmmm."

"You know what? I went out on a date with a friend of my husband's, he's great, we had a fantastic time."

"Well there it is then. You can marry him," I said to her, and screw *me* over as usual, I thought.

"No way. It's my husband's friend."

Then she told me that since she had started fighting with her engineer he had had two accidents, totaling two cars, and had even shot himself once when he was drunk, that they had been sleeping in separate bedrooms for the last two months and that she hadn't made love with anyone. "I'm never going to make love with you again," she said to me. "You can count on it."

"Me neither. It's not worth getting a bit of ass just so you can fuck me over again. You are the most selfish person on earth," I told her.

While I said this she had started trimming my moustache; I felt like I was being castrated. She also wanted to cut my nails, my beard, my hair. To leave me clean and healthy. She told me her engineer took fourteen showers a day.

I thought about the theory that when people die their nails keep growing. Then I remembered another theory that says that it's not that dead people's nails grow, but that their skin dries up, and it looks like they're growing only because you can see the part that used to be under the skin. I remembered the clever novels that Onetti wrote. I remembered that if I wasn't a genius it didn't matter if my nails were cut. I pulled my hand away from her scissors. "Why are you so determined to cut something off my body?" I asked her. She laughed. I saw a woman in the distance who looked like Carolina and I felt like crying. "So why did you and Carolina break up?" she asked.

"Because she slept with five guys before she met me."

"You're very sick."

"Could be."

"And you weren't jealous about it when you were with me?"

"You never gave me a chance. You would have told me to fuck off. But then again, you did anyway. We always end up sending each other to hell. We were never happy."

"Don't start with that bullshit," she said. I noticed she was starting to get some gray hairs, at thirty-one years old.

"You're right, it's bullshit."

"Anyway," she added, "I can say things to make you feel bad, too."

Everything was becoming so stupid. I wandered through life like an imbecile, surrounded by all the smog that filtered down among the flowers of the clock, advancing irremediably toward the abortion.

Who Farted?

So there I was, untalented, without even having correctly timed the twenty-eight days in which my great novel took place; instead I kept collapsing or stretching it out in this raw, crude, oxytocin-filled manuscript, born of a bewitched uterus, where I see my face bathed in dark, black blood.

It was the abortive blood of Carolina, the bloody black threads of Pamela, the incinerated fingernails of my father, the fiery look of my brother who wouldn't look at me anymore, and the rope that wound itself around me there in the park, leaving me to drown me in my own insides.

I remembered I used to like talking to my insides, that every morning I would try to hold up my face that was melting over my impotence. "So. Are you coming with me to my analyst?"

"Okay, okay, I'll go with you."

We looked for the entrance to the park and on the way to the car she said, "But we're going in your car. In *your* car."

"Yes, Pamela. I know you don't lift a fucking finger for anyone. You're a spoiled brat, just like me."

"You know what? Maybe I shouldn't go with you."

"Whatever you want."

When we got to the sidewalk she said to me, her eyes rubbed raw by the smog: "Let's go. But we're going in your car."

"Yes, Pamela. Whatever you say."

I turned on the radio when we got into the car; they were announcing that 1,534 people had died in Camaroon from a volcanic eruption that had released toxic gases. I felt ridiculous for being miserable because I was a bad writer, for crying for my father's death, for feeling that my penis had been abandoned among the noise, smog, and castrating women. Then more news: Mexico would need ten billion dollars to offset the negative impact of the fall in oil prices. "It's been almost a year since the earthquake," Pamela said.

"Yeah."

More news: They had discovered a warehouse with twenty-eight tons of marijuana; it was to be burned by the authorities. I suddenly felt like I had to fart, one of those big, dry farts that send a shivery chill down your spine. Since I no longer had any confidence in her, I let it out bit by bit, opening the window so she wouldn't smell it, but she smelled it anyway. "Did you just fart?" she asked me.

"No," I said. "It just smells bad around here. Better close the window."

She closed it and I farted again. I had closed my window too.

"Jesus Christ! The smell already got in!" I said.

"Yeah," she said.

Then she heard me giggling and realized that I was the one stinking up the place. She opened the window, sticking her head out so the air would go up her nose. She was sitting with her head outside the car, cracking up; she loved the joke I had played and she tried to make herself fart, too. "If you keep straining like that you're going to shit in your pants," I smiled at her, giving her my best playboy look.

Being Famous is a Pain in the Ass

"How's it going with your book?" she asked me.

"Pretty well, better than I thought it would."

"Is that good?"

"The newspaper reviews have been pretty favorable. And there are some people who want to meet me. I don't know what they want."

"Have you sold many copies?"

"More or less. A lot of bookstores refused it. I guess the cover with the girl showing her nipples scares them. In certain bookstores that doesn't surprise me. But they didn't want it at the 'cool' bookstores, and that seemed kinda strange. There must be a lot of people who want to avoid any possible problems and so they just say no. I even talked to Galíndez, the head of distribution, and he told me they'll accept any book—except mine. They treat suppliers like they were bums begging for change. You know how it is, they're still waiting for the last unpublished story by Borges. They probably think I'm dirty."

"Or a bad writer."

"Maybe. But the only thing the buyers read is *Reader's Digest*. They'll only order what people ask them for and people don't ask for sex until a nipple touches their skin and they feel the first impact of desire."

"Freud said that all pleasure that isn't continuous provokes displeasure."

"Exactly. Besides, you have to be named García Márquez or José Agustín to see your book on a good table."

"What's a good table?"

"Where people can see it. But for that you have to get down on your knees in front of the buyers, stick out your tongue, open their zippers and lick their balls, making sure you don't pull any hair; you have to give them continuous pleasure so they stay hot; that's how you can get into a bookstore; but then even though they're foaming at the mouth because it feels so good they send you to hell anyway. That's why I'd rather sell them on the street. But that's also a drag because people don't trust the cover. It's a drag."

"Do you make a lot of money?"

"The distributor gives me a hundred pesos per book."

"So by the year 2100 you'll be a millionaire."

"Yeah. But I don't care if my books sell or not."

"What do you want then?"

"I want someone in a bar to read my book and feel the same way I felt when I was writing it."

We were going about forty miles an hour.

"Fine, but you're not García Márquez or Borges."

"I know. But they're not me, either."

"Give me a break."

"Oh well, now go to hell, up yer ass so you can't pass gas."

We were on the freeway outside the city and we slowed to ten miles an hour. Most of the cars had just one person inside. In their laminated fish tanks, with their throats dried up, our only communication was honking at each other. "Hey, why is it so important to be famous?" Pamela asked me.

"So people will love me and give me a joint now and then."

"That's it?"

"No. I also want to be able to piss on the sidewalk and have people say,

'We saw a Nobel prizewinner pissing on the sidewalk!'"

"Fascinating. Are you still writing your new novel? What was it called?" she asked, as if it would do any good to talk about it.

"*Doggie Style*."

"Well, what do you expect? You scare people with your titles."

"I was going to call it *A Dog's Life*, but I liked *Doggie Style* better." I braked suddenly; a car with some undercover cops was passing me. I wanted to scream at them but my preservation instinct and my reality principle stopped me. "Did you make up with your brother yet?"

"He hasn't made up with me."

"What would you like to be doing right now?"

"Making love with Carolina."

"Do you really love her? More than you love me?"

"After this fucking interview, yes. But soon I'm going to stop loving altogether."

"When?"

"Maybe when I put the finishing touches on the novel I'm writing, or when I find someone else, or when she sleeps with someone else, when I'm finally filled with hate, when I've gotten over my father's death. I don't know—but I am going to stop loving altogether."

"Are you sure?"

"I just stopped being in love with you."

"Why?"

"Because you want to get married again and you tell me as though it wouldn't even matter to me."

"Would you marry me?"

"If we had taken your car, yes. But too late, you fucked up."

"So anyway, what do you learn in your writing workshops?"

"To write like everyone else."

"Oh. And you write differently?"

"No."

"So, why do you keep doing it?"

"To stop from killing myself."

"Oh, I see."

"Hey," I asked her, "did you know that the farts you can't hear are the ones that stink? And the ones that don't stink are always really loud?"

"So what does that mean?"

"That there's no salvation. You're fucked either way."

"Aaahh. There's no salvation."

"No."

Return to Regressions

We got to the office. I gave her my keys and told her to be back for me in exactly fifty minutes.

It's in a modern building with gray stairs. The waiting room has a little buzzer you ring so the analyst will know you're there, ready to lie down on the couch. Ready for punctuation, ready to believe that your words will come back to you, inverted. To have someone who'll listen to you. How do the working class and the *campesinos* manage without psychoanalysis? My friend José Luis, the Lacanian, says that after Freud came along the number of suicides decreased. Could that be true? This didn't help me at all; my quest was to finish my novel so I could kill myself in peace. "If my books live on, then death doesn't matter," Simone de Beauvoir said.

In the waiting room there are magazines where the more psychopathic of us draw fangs on the pictures of Reagan and Thatcher.

In the dentist's office next door you could hear Napoleón singing, "They are the most beautiful of God's creation. I would happily give my other rib, they are a box filled with surprises and we feel lost when they leave us. Woooomeeeen, we will swallow our pride for woooomeeeen." Holy shit! I need a joint.

I was suddenly aware that I had smoked an entire pack of cigarettes; my tongue was trapped by a scratchy fabric that covered my little-used mucous membranes. What must my lungs look like? Like shit. That's great! I love being self-destructive. Carolina had never called me back and I felt that the earth would open up, swallowing my anxieties. It was difficult for me to breathe in such a romantic and asthmatic state. I clasped my hands, rubbing the sweat together.

I rang the buzzer to let the other patient know I was there and that he could just go to hell, that it was my turn to talk about all my bullshit and to lament over my 'a' object; that is, the object of my longing.

But was it really the object of my longing, or was everything an illusory theory? I must really believe in Freud, if I'm willing to pay ten thousand pesos for fifty minutes and to explore the repulsive world of my brain where the truth is never told.

While I was waiting, I picked up a newspaper's arts section, and right in front of me was a poem by Jaroslav Seifert called 'Spring in the Fisherman's Net.' The last two stanzas were great. I read them about ten times so I would remember them, but finally I tore the page out. There in that poem was the sea I had lost in Carolina's body, my broken dreams and my brilliant stupidity. It went like this:

In the fisherman's net fringed with cork,
the wind was trapped. Its smile
is the smile that all women know
when they speak of men among themselves.

In the fisherman's net fringed with cork,
the small claws held a fragile fear
still alive. This is the fear that men know
when they speak of women among themselves.

I lit another cigarette, thinking that with these verses I could end my great novel, but I preferred to light another cigarette, a sign that I still had a body left to destroy. I didn't stop smoking even for a minute.

Finally the door opened. A man about four and a half feet tall who looked like Yoda from *Star Wars* held his fleshy and veined hand out to me.

I went in without looking at his face and settled myself onto the couch. I relaxed; after twenty leaden seconds of blue smoke I said to him: "Well, um, turns out Carolina told me to fuck off."

Then I was quiet. On the other side of the window there was some construction work going on; a construction worker was hanging outside from the twentieth floor. I imagined how horrible it would be to be hung-over on a job like that. "Besides," I went on, "Pamela's waiting for me outside. Can you believe it? She's getting a divorce so she can marry someone she hasn't met yet."

"Hmmmm," Yoda said, which I interpreted as, "What a bitch!"

"Can you believe it, doctor?"

He didn't say anything. Some whiny Indian raga was running through my brain.

I thought I should talk about my father's death instead of asses, anuses and vaginas. The pain of my suffering confused my neural synapses, as if they couldn't make contact, as if I were incapable of stringing together another metaphor in my life. I need a joint, I thought. Holy Mother, how I need a joint! Would it be possible to get that here, too? "What are you thinking about?" a voice asked that came from behind me. A voice without a face, like the exit from beyond the grave.

"That I really need to smoke some pot. Well, okay, I don't physically need it, but psychologically I do." I was embarrassed by my denial. Should I try to justify myself? Which of the many psychoanalysis books was he thinking about now? Which one was it? Melanie Klein, or Anna Freud? Maybe there was some anti-psychiatrist who would justify my behavior. Or maybe he was thinking about Jacques Lacan. No, not Lacan; the association he belongs to rejects Lacan. Still, maybe that's who he was thinking of. "What are you thinking about?" he asked me again.

"Well, I'm wondering what you're thinking about."

He didn't say anything, and then I said, "Doctor, Carolina died. You know what I mean? She died, that daughter of a fucking bitch." I forgot he was there. "She died. She'll never be back and if she does she'll be just like Pamela: perforated by another man, dripping semen, and anyway she'll only come back for revenge, demanding that I give her her self-esteem back." I felt I was intellectualizing here. "They only come back to screw us over. And still it's as if they weren't really back at all; they stay trapped in their hate and they'll say I only know how to talk about two things: jealousy and alcohol."

This is why Carolina told me to fuck off. She left me because I'm an imbecile.

I felt like I should be talking about my father's death. But how does one talk about something like that? Should I say how I still felt his hand holding mine, embracing me with his cold nicotine-stained fingers? A strong hand that supported me with all the coldness of his skin? How can I talk about this? It was way too intimate. How could this interest my analyst?

In the building across the street two more construction workers were hanging out the window. "Poor guys! They don't have psychoanalysts," I thought. "What are you thinking about?" he asks me.

"About my father and about the fact that I'm a spoiled rich kid. About that I'm one of the few intellectuals who have a psychoanalyst, well, at least, who have the money to pay for one."

Talk about my father? I was the one who had to carry his ashes. Even though I never saw them, I believed everyone who said they were inside the heavy box that looked like a safe. An urn fit for Scrooge McDuck, one that my father would have made fun of. Or who knows? In his time, having money was the greatest triumph. It's the same way now for those who don't have it. My goal in life was to achieve the courage to kill myself or to find the phrase that would convince me once and for all of the existence of God.

I didn't want to talk about my father. I wanted to tell the analyst that I was going to call Carolina and that she would come back to the apartment to wait for me with some fish and lots of garlic. "Hmmm," said the doctor, waiting for me to speak.

"You know what, doctor? I'm sure that the man who hates me most in the world is my brother. But he doesn't even know it. If he knew, maybe he would stop. No, I don't believe I'm inventing anything. It's true, because I hate him, I envy him: my mother opened her legs to give birth to him before me."

"One time," I went on, "when he had his first singing recital, I bought a copy of *Duda* magazine and I sat down in the front row and instead of watching him and listening to him sing I read the magazine. I was afraid he would screw up. That bothered him; he never forgave me, but he also never asked me why I did it."

A construction worker is signaling another.

"Doctor, goddamn Pamela wants to marry someone else. She knows it's impossible for us to get married. She knows I can't deal with her pampered little girl tone of voice, and she knows she couldn't deal with my going on and on about jealousy and alcohol. Pamela is dead, doctor. Dead. If I hadn't seen her again she would still be alive, but now she's dead."

"Tell me, doctor, what went wrong with Carolina? I know analysts hate it when their patients ask them direct questions, but tell me, what went wrong?"

"Well," he said, arranging his throat to surround the words he was about to say, "what sometimes happens is that when one has an important loss, other people begin to slip through our hands."

"They get afraid of our demand for affection?"

"That's more or less it."

More or less? I remembered that a teacher of psychoanalysis I once had, someone who belonged to the same association as this man behind me, told me that my analyst was A TOTAL JERK.

"What are you thinking about?"

"About when I was drunk one time and I called Dr. Navarrete on the phone at three in the morning and he told me you were a jerk."

Yoda starting laughing.

Then the fifty minutes had gone by, and with a blade that cut off all further language he said, "Okay ...." This 'okay' meant that time was up. I would see him in the next session. Meanwhile he would wait for his next patient, one perhaps—hopefully—more fucked up than I. Maybe a schizophrenic. I got up from the couch, went towards the door, and returned the padded handshake with which he had received me. I left thinking, this jerk won't get Carolina back for me. Fuck it!

You Just Gotta Go For It, Man

I left the office; there was Pamela waiting for me with her new gray hairs. At one time I had left a sliver of my heart between her legs.

I got into the car. "I'm cured!" I said. She laughed. We went to get her car. I didn't feel like saying anything, what I would have told her didn't matter anyway. Instead, I thought about Irma and Javier. Javier was a buddy of mine, a real tyrannical bastard. When he was fifteen he had told his father to go fuck himself, and he went to work to support his brothers and sisters himself. "My father was a lazy ass, that's why I did it," Javier would say. Then he fell in love with Irma, who was married. He climbed on top of her and they did it doggie style; even after he got her pregnant he kept screwing her without saying anything to the husband, who was sat around drinking all day. The end of the story is like so many others. Irma was afraid to tell her husband the truth, so she pretended nothing had happened, and returned to her security. In a few years they'll know who the father is.

Her aunts and some other ladies say it's the husband's. No one knows, nobody knew about the daily events that finally ended in hate and betrayal. Poor Javier, all I could say to him was, "You just gotta go for it, man. Nothing else matters."

I left Pamela at her car. I went back to my apartment, called my mother and she told me some warts had popped up on her face, caused by some medicine she had been taking for a while; she said they were probably cancerous. We hung up.

That was all I needed, for my mother to have cancer of the face. My God, how do the poor survive without psychoanalysts!

Even though everything and nothing was irremediable, I felt lost. I fell face down on my bed. Worst of all, my dick was hard and there was no one around to fuck. To masturbate would have dragged me to an even deeper pit of guilt and solitude. I could go to Alcoholics Anonymous for a bit. Although they had saved me for four months, the longest I had ever gone without drinking, I felt different from them. I recalled them in a phrase by Rabelais in *Gargantua and Pantagruel*: "When there is a wall in front of you and a wall behind you, the whispering, the envy, the mutual conspiracy is all around you." But, oh well, there was no other way, I had to climb into the AA boat so I wouldn't fall off the wagon.

Lying in bed, horny. A bored rich boy, feeling the thorns of the worst *fleurs du mal.* Alienated and stupefied by men and by women, I would fall once more into my own insides. That's when Mike called. "Hey, man, what's going on? Wanna go to Guacatitlán? We're going to hear some rock."

"Okay. I'll call Rogelio."

I dialed Rogelio's number. "What's happening man? You want to go to Guacatitlán?"

"I can't," he whispered. "I have a girl in my bed."

"Just like someone probably has Carolina right now," I thought.

"What's her name?" I asked.

"Talia."

"So what's the story?"

"Not much, she came on to me at an office party. She works for the phone company."

"So how's it going, did you do it doggie style yet?"

"Oh man, if you were only here to see it. I thought she was gonna be a prude, and when I looked up, there she was, naked and in bed. She didn't want to do anything and ended up asking me to show her my dick. She saw it and then climbed on top of it like an Amazon. It's incredible!"

"So has she worn you out yet?"

"Yep. So what's with you? Listen, I'm gonna go finish screwing."

"Bye. Get in an extra one for me."

Little Fish

I grabbed the telephone, overwhelmed by the fear that my anxiety would return. I called Carolina's number and Hosco answered. "Look, stop bothering my daughter. She's already made a report to the police about you. She doesn't want to see you anymore. You're a sick person." Hosco had returned from his weekend with his daughter. He was right in wanting to protect her, I would have done the same thing. "Besides, young man, it seems very strange to me. There are a lot of fish in the sea. You're young, you have your whole life ahead of you." I didn't say anything; if he was going to give me advice maybe he saw something bad in her that I hadn't detected. And I thought: "Of course! He's right, I'll go look for another little fish." I immediately called Mike. "Let's go to Guacatitlán."

Guacatitlán

We got to the club; luckily we had smoked some herb on the way. We went in and I saw a group of girls sitting at a table, drinking and looking pretty for all the men; a lot of people were shouting along with the band but no one had dared to get up to dance.

"How strange," I thought, "all these guys used to be 'revolutionaries' and now they're embarrassed to request a José José song, even though that's what they really like." Outside there was some commotion because a gang of rowdies were trying to get in and they were being stopped at the door. There were plenty of girls, but how could I get at them in the middle of all these low tables without making myself look ridiculous? Without wanting to be, we were all caught in the same mock politeness. Holy Christ!

Luckily, there were two girls sitting near us and both of them had beautiful tits. I couldn't resist the temptation and I went up to them. "Hi," I said.

"Hi." We immediately liked each other and I sat down. That was when the devil appeared in front of me, disguised in the shape of a bottle of white wine.

The girls were pretty loaded; they didn't have to insist much for me to drink my first glass. Before I knew it I had a glass in front of me that thrust up a cold, thin liquid. I drank it without thinking. I forgot all about Alcoholics Anonymous, I forgot that I shouldn't ever forget. And I began to feel good. Immediately after that I started to worry about the supply of alcohol. "What? You're drinking?" Mike said to me. "Holy shit! You're going to go crazy."

"Not true. I'm just having a few drinks."

"A FEW DRINKS?"

Yeah, why not? I was going to go crazy; I wanted to reach above the sheets of mysticism, to swallow all the shit I hadn't been able to spit out, to raise my eyelids to the sky, to touch the neon light with my insides, above the live flesh, to destroy my body, to bleed it dry and present it to my father.

I suddenly remembered that I was sitting next to four breasts. I looked at them cynically. How many civilizations had gone by in order to create these breasts? Had Napoleon seen them? Had Anaximander kissed them? Or some slave? What was I doing at Guacatitlán? Who are we? Where are we going? Where is the umbilical cord of the world? Who created kitsch? Why did William Burroughs die? Why doesn't anyone tell the truth?

In the sixties I never imagined that I'd make it to the seventies; it's the same thing now with the eighties. Oh, Mike, I'm sorry—I can't write *A Hundred Years of Solitude.*

One of the girls got up to go to the bathroom; she had a lovely, swinging behind. My mind was drawn to her, reflecting the neon lights of my eyes against her jean-wrapped ass.

I reached my hand toward a plastic glass filled with white wine, drinking it carefully so I wouldn't smash the cup, but it spilled anyway on the way to my mouth. I felt everyone looking at me like I was a drunk, but they were drunk too, and their white and mocking teeth chewed away at my pleasure. I remembered a friend once saying to me, "This isn't living, this is really living!"

Oh, Marcel Proust, why aren't you here with me? You were bourgeois, too. We would understand each other, we would join together so the Marxists could hate us. Oh, Prince Kropotkin, why aren't you here with me? You would teach me what it is I must do. Oh, Lenin, why aren't you here with me? Oh, Lowry, why aren't you here with me? Oh, Christ, why aren't you here with me? Forgive me, Father; I know not what I do.

I came out of my reverie of nostalgia and happiness and melancholy deliberation and tedious dialogue. How beautiful it is to drink, to feel my throat lightened and refreshed, to note without denoting how my brain was deadened, lost in a magic placidity, as if my genital organs soothed and covered the whole world with their warm scrotum. In this moment I loved the whole world, everything and everyone.

I loved all the dogs who wake me up with their barking, all the dogs lying crushed at the curb, a dog dead of starvation, I loved them all, even the dead ones, those I loved even more—they were the reason for my existence; there was nothing more extraordinary than loving and living for the dead, searching them out in their worm-eaten tomb, checking to make sure their balls were still there so they could become great men, great dead men.

One of the girls spilled some wine on her shirt, you could see an erect nipple underneath, a delectable and procreant nipple. This breast would be mine tonight, I would suck it and suck it until I was born again, until I could throw off the rope that was around my neck, until I was rid of the reality that smothered me. It was a beautiful nipple; I didn't know if it was brown or pink. I had had many surprises in this area. I don't know of any man who can guess the color of a woman's nipple. I approached her provocatively. "Can I suck you?" I said in a drunken voice. And Mike shoved me in the head. "You're smashed, aren't you, jackass?" he said, smiling.

"Yes, Mike."

"Hey," he said, spraying spit into my mouth as he talked; he had to scream because of the music, "I think your novel *Doggie Style* shouldn't end with all the characters screwing doggie style. It's too forced."

"I know, Mike, I already knew that. This novel has no end. Well, hic, yes it has an end, but I don't know what it is yet, it could come any time."

Then the music got really crazy. "But don't blame rock for what goes on in this plaaaace!" they sang.

Some guy sitting alone at a table was playing drums in the air in front of him. "Did you see how great that bastard plays the drums?" I said to Mike.

"Yeah, far out. Hey," he said, spraying his stupid spit all over my face, "do you want the one with the big tits or the one with the ass?"

"The one with the big tits and the ass."

"Cut the crap, come on, really."

"Well let's flip for it, let's be civilized about it, we'll trade off. You know how girls are these days. Since they know the bomb could drop any day they'll drop their pants for anyone."

"I'm not interested in your social theories."

"Fine, well I'll take the big breasts. But then we'll trade, okay?"

"Okay."

So Here I Am, Between Two Tits

The music stopped and we started talking to the girls. "I'm a dancer," one of them said.

"I'm into literature," said the other.

"I'm a painter," Mike said.

"What do you do?" they asked me.

"Me? Well, um, well, I write," I said, feeling very small.

"Oh, you write? What do you write?"

"Dirty novels."

"Ohh," said the one with the ass.

I stood up drunkenly and screamed, "PLAY SOME JOSE JOSEEEEEE!"

"Sit down!" Mike shouted at me. "They're going to throw you out!"

"So what, man, I want to hear a song by José José."

"Shut up you geek from the seventies. They'll throw you out!"

I sat down, really pissed off that I had to sit there suffering through blasts of electronic music with no beat. I got up again. "PLAY SOME BEEEGEEEEEES!" Mike pulled me down by the shoulder. "Please, please shut up."

"Fuck you, Mike! I want to hear a song by John Travolta. Don't you know I'm going to be in the *Saturday Night Fever* contest?"

"Yeah, buddy, but no one cares."

The music changed, they put on something with more rhythm. Then I brushed my knee against one of the girls'. Oooh, delicious!—went my heart.

Mike had already dropped his hand and placed it on the other girl's ass. The one with the tits began to nibble at the corner of my lips and pushed and pulled her tongue out like she was looking for mine. "Mmm, I like it," she purred, "you taste like wine."

"I'm in Alcoholics Anonymous," I said.

"Forget Alcoholics Anonymous."

She brought her hand to the glass. She raised it toward my mouth and fed me a wonderful wine that tickled my salivary glands, making my scalp bristle. With her other hand she grabbed the hair on the back of my neck and I felt a delightful tug on the head of my penis. She put the glass down on the table and started rubbing her hand against my balls. On the way, she caressed my inner thigh with her fingernail. I was starting to get hard and I raised myself up a little in my seat to rearrange things inside my pants.

Mike was kissing the one with the ass; I watched her tongue going over his shaved cheek, leaving it shiny with pleasure-seeking saliva. "Hey," I said to the girl who was with me, "what's your name?"

"Livia," she answered.

"No, really."

"Why don't you believe me?"

"And what's your friend's name?"

"Paty."

I grabbed Mike's shoulder. "You hear that, Mike? The girl you're kissing is named Paty."

"So what?" he said.

"I once had a girlfriend named Paty."

"So? Is this her?"

"No."

"So what then?"

"Well, nothing, really."

"Fine, now take care of your own, fer chrissake."

Livia was now grabbing my balls with a tenderness reserved for bitches and their puppies. My penis was getting fatter and getting stuck in my pants; it was really painful. I straightened up a little, but the seats were so low, the only way to get comfortable was by taking it out completely. "Hey, Mike, this is uncomfortable," I said.

"I know."

"Let's go to Rogelio's apartment. We can crash at his place."

"Nah, he'll freak. Let's go to yours."

"No way. Don't you know that a certain girl's father is on the lookout for me?"

"Are you serious?"

"Very. They left a message with Floyd."

"Who's Floyd?"

"A machine that answers my telephone."

"Okay, so let's go to Rogelio's. But if he throws us out we'll go to your house."

"Or to your apartment."

"No, we're going to yours, you're the rich one; if we go to mine you'll do something stupid and then they'll kick me out. I, for one, have to work."

"Cool."

What is Life?

On the way to Rogelio's house my mind was wandering, as usual. At that moment the police could be looking for me to hold me responsible for all the madness in the world. It was easy for them, all they had to do was to stick some drugs down your pants and then send you off to jail. Or even better, they could indict me for not having cried at my father's grave, like Mersault in *The Stranger*. Just like him, I would ask that a lot of people go to my execution so they could scream out all the hate they held toward me.

A car full of undercover police passed in front of us. I knew these were my last days, that I would die of something sudden.

This chapter could remain unfinished, my life could be squashed into streams of blood by some gorilla cops or maybe I'll just be gunned down. Like Rogelio once said, we only live until someone finally gives the order: "KILL THE BASTARD!" And then, of course, I would be with my father, with the dead, with Lowry, with the millions of Russians killed by the Nazis, twenty-two million to be almost exact.

I'll die from doing something stupid, and then everyone will want to claim their share, everyone except my mother; she'll just cry and stop believing in the people she never believed in.

And Carolina? Will she wait for me on the other side of autumn? And Pamela? And my psychoanalyst? And my brother? And my sister?

Everything will be erased in the moment I crash and am engraved against a police car at sixty miles an hour. Dostoyevsky at least had a minute to look around before his execution. In the end they didn't execute him anyway, but he used that minute well. My death will have an impact; at least two or three tabloids will write about it. My body will collapse into itself, lost between my own two hands that can no longer support it. I'll see my father again between the blood, snot and tears. I'll be cremated, too, and will request that everyone come shout at me, the people who hated me as well as the ones I hated.

Forgive me, Father; I know not what I do.

I will die from sex.

I will die from smog.

I will die from pamphlets about being alcoholic.

I look in the rear view mirror, Mike's busy making out and I say, my thoughts unsteady, as if my neurons had been intercepted by menstrual blood, or better yet, as if I had burst an artery and could never again create a metaphor, "Mike! MIKE! I'm sorry, I can't write *A Hundred Years of Solitude*."

"Is this the end?" he asks me.

"It's the end."

"That's it, no more sex?"

"No more sex."

"Damn!"

Epilogue with García Márquez
My dream come true: I am Pavlov's dog

Writing this is like having to plunge straight into a cold swimming pool.

Since I'm supposedly Pavlov's dog it's been difficult to find the right background music (silence would be all wrong).

But who is Pavlov's dog? (Pavlov isn't a dog.)

Dr Pavlov had a little dog and each time he fed it he'd ring a bell. Then ol' Pavlov tied the poor thing up and stuck some wires on it to watch how its gastric juices would flow every time he rang the bell, even without the smell or sight of food: this is how conditioning was born.

Since I'm still preparing for the dive, I have to find some eighties music (Jesus, the eighties have been going on forever): Phil Collins, Rod Stewart, *Promesas* by José José, techno rock, Las Insólitas Imágenes de Aurora, El Tri, Maldita Vecindad y los Hijos del Quinto Patio, The Cars, etc.

Another problem is that from my spot on the diving board I can see a guy at the side of the pool looking at me, and this guy is named Gabriel García Márquez. Even though this is all in my imagination, I see him sitting in a bathing suit, drinking a tall drink through a straw. He's watching me, smiling as if to say: "Go ahead! Dive in, you bastard."

And I have to take the plunge.

Flashback. Run the tape, pal:

I needed a preface for this book.

A preface by García Márquez.

Simply because García Márquez won the Nobel Prize.

If I got a preface from him for my book, it would be—why not say it?—like winning the lottery.

That's right! I'd get a preface from him and I'd become rich and famous: the ultimate petit-bourgeois dream ....

Borges says being rich is the most vulgar banality of all.

Well, I wanted to be famous like everyone else (sorry, Marxists!).

It all happened on October 3.

A while back Mongo had told me, "Hey, García Márquez is going to dedicate some commemorative plaque for *Espejos*, the play Gurrola's directing. Why don't you go try to nab him there and tell him to write a preface for your book? It would be like winning the lottery."

"Like winning the lottery. Exactly."

The idea kept rolling around in my head, just like it would to anyone else who hears fame knocking at the door.

Since I was more interested in my novel than in the preface I didn't take it too seriously. "Anyway," I joked to myself, "if García Márquez won't do it, I'll see if I can find Onetti." And bang!—I was asleep.

Then October 3 came. I felt like one of those teenage girls who win a contest and get a date with their favorite singer; that night would be my 'dream come true'.

"To dreeeeeam the impossible dreeeeam."

That moron Rogelio gave me the wrong address, although he got me to more or less the right neighborhood. He had said it was in La Capilla theater. I was late, so I jumped out of the car and said to the guy at the ticket booth:

"One, please."

"It's 1500 pesos."

"Hey, is García Márquez here yet?"

"García Márquez?" He looked at me like I was crazy.

"Yeah, García Márquez. He's coming to dedicate a plaque. Isn't Gurrola's play on here?"

"No."

"Where is it?"

"At the Santa Catarina."

"Thanks."

It was a good thing I hadn't bought a ticket. "Rogelio's a fucking idiot," I thought on the way back to the car. "And so am I."

I got back into the car, in the night and the rain. (I had almost bought the wrong lottery ticket and sat down to see some strange play and of course I would have shit in my pants from the horror and stupidity of it.)

I ask five people how to get to the goddamn fucking Santa Catarina Theater. (I was really pissed off. I had cancelled a trip to eat peyote in Valle de Bravo for this.)

I knew I was lost, and I kept circling around Coyoacán, wondering where on earth I could find Onetti, and then finally a woman told me: "It's right here, around the corner." I turned the corner and parked the car, bringing along a copy of my earlier book, *Doll, Do Me a Favor and Take Off Your Bra*, to give García Márquez.

In the agony of looking for the theater his name started growing bigger in my mind and I repeated to myself: Fernando, they're going to call you an *arriviste*. Like I give a shit. I walked over to the door of the theater and found Mongo, who was feeling cocky because his girlfriend appeared naked in the play (not completely, she only showed her tits). "Hey," I asked him, "doesn't it make you jealous that your girlfriend's up on stage like that? Don't bullshit me, you know how jealous you are."

"Big deal. My mother was a cabaret dancer."

"Oh. Listen, is García Márquez here yet?"

"No."

"What kind of car is he coming in?"

"In a Nobel," he answered.

I congratulated him on his stupid joke and we went into the theater.

I sat down behind some reserved seats. "They're going to sit there for sure and I'll get him from behind," I thought. "I want that lottery! Yaaaaay!! Long live García Márquez!"

Then the play started; I loved it. The problem was the first act took hours and I really had to pee. I sat in a thousand different positions trying to get rid of that awful sensation. When there was enough light I looked at the faces of the others who were also shifting their asses around in their seats, trying to keep them from falling asleep, or maybe they were holding in a fart or they had to piss. "Damn," I thought, "could this be one of old Gurrola's jokes? I'm sitting here, dying to take a leak and this motherfucker García Márquez isn't showing up. Shit."

Finally the first act ended.

I said to the guy next to me: "Save my seat."

I ran to look for the bathroom.

The theater is connected to a restaurant that's in the same building. In order to pee I had to pass through this restaurant that was all wood, Pierre Cardin and wine, in short, a restaurant for intellectual yuppies like me.

On the way to the bathroom, as I went through a doorway, I saw a man who was eating and staring at the wall and at his wife. It was García

Márquez. No shit! I recognized him from all the pictures I've seen. It was him!

I forgot all about the bathroom and went to get the book that I had left in my seat in the theater. I grabbed it and went back to the Nobel Prize.

Without thinking I walked up to him, held out my hand and said, trying to be as funny as possible: "Hi, Gabriel, I'm the wizard Cannabis."

"Look I only need ten seconds. I just finished writing the *A Hundred Years of Solitude* of the eighties and I need you to write me a preface."

"Sit down."

As I sat down at the table his Nobel halo covered me and I prayed to God that all my unappreciative ex-girlfriends and all the intellectuals who had called me a drunk would pass by and I, smiling, would say to them: "Hi, girls, hi guys, well, you see, I'm here with Gabo planning our next novel. Later when I get some time I'll call you. Okay. Bye. Don't bother coming over here. Euwww, it smells bad in here, someone get rid of them."

"I brought a book for you to read. See if you like it."

He took the book and gave it to a woman who I guessed was his wife.

A well-dressed man walked in and came up to him. I'll draw a plan of where we were sitting and who we were.

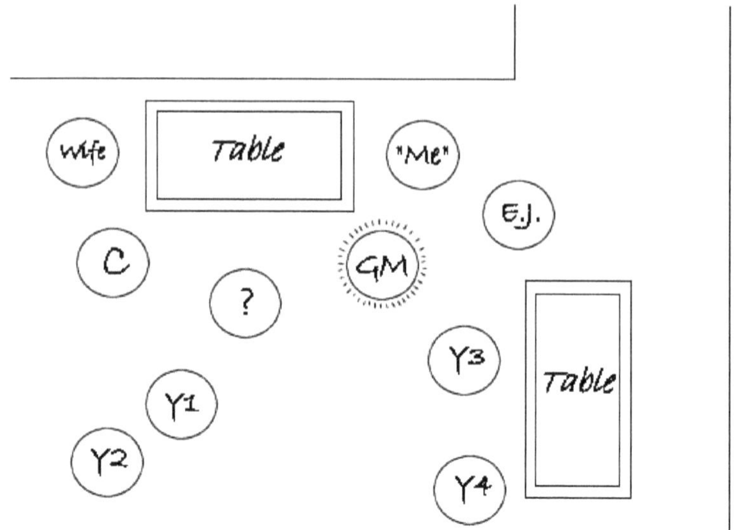

Jesus. Let me try to sort out this mess.

Y1 and Y2 are two women sitting behind Gabo; they're 'Yuppie 1' and 'Yuppie 2'.

The 'C' stands for Colombian. I didn't know anything else about her, but she was beautiful. You'll see a question mark in the diagram; that corresponds to a fat, gray-haired man. He was pretty cool. I knew he had an important job because at one point during the conversation he said so, but I never found out what it was; I think it was vice-consul of something or vice-president of some company or other.

But why should I worry, if sitting to my left was the Nobel himself. That's right! Look at me now, you intellectuals from Jalapa. Ha, ha, ha! I am sitting to the right of the president of Macondo, ha, ha, ha, and soon the world will be mine, ha, ha, ha.

Then there's a place occupied by an 'E.J.' That's the space for the Ever-Present Journalists. There was no chair there, only the embarrassment of standing in the aisle bugging the waiters just so they could touch Gabo.

All right guys! Don't touch. Ooh, it smells bad in here.

There are also some numbers. Those are for the yuppies at the other tables, eating and talking in a low voice and looking out of the corner of their eyes at García Márquez. Every now and then one of them was bold enough to say to his girlfriend:

"Listen—go walk towards the bathroom; García Márquez is over there around the corner."

"No, you go. I'm too embarrassed."

As you'll see in the diagram there is a character that says WIFE. This is very important; she represents a fascinating extension of the Nobel. You could call her the feminine half of the prize. A princess from Macondo, or simply the woman García Márquez sleeps with.

The wall plays a very important role. It allows Gabo to look straight ahead without worrying about who's staring at him. This helps him to relax.

When he was still working on his steak, an Ever-Present Journalist came over.

"Sir, why haven't you allowed me an interview?"

"I don't know," García Márquez said. "Maybe I just don't like you."

"But sir, at least let me watch you write. Just let me come in. I'll do the rest."

"And don't you want to watch me go to the bathroom?" Gabo answered.

At that I asked his wife: "Excuse me, do you know where the peepee room is?"

"Outside on your right."

I felt tired as I went out. Luckily the bathroom was empty and all mine. I pointed toward the urinal, unzipped my fly, and pulled out a piece of watery meat; it was my penis. I began to relax my mind and my sphincter, and playfully began pissing around some little holes. I shook four times when I was done. I zipped my pants carefully so I wouldn't catch any hairs, looked at myself in the mirror and said: I've bought my lottery ticket, now I have to win it. But what the fuck do I say to Gabo so he'll understand how important it is that Carolina and Pamela see a preface by him and how much joy it would bring me? Goddamn it. What do I say?

I left the bathroom afraid that the journalist had taken my seat next to the throne. Luckily he hadn't. I would have kicked his ass out of there!

I sat down, happy. I lit a cigarette and smoked it nervously; lately I've been pissing more nicotine than water. My lungs are headed straight for the sewer.

Finally García Márquez got rid of the intruders.

"May I ask you something or do you want me to go?" I said to him, now feeling sure of myself.

"No, man. Order a lemonade."

A LEMONADE! No shit! I told you, Raimundo Mier! I told you! García Márquez is right on.

I called the waiter over scornfully, just to test how far the ultrasonic rays of the Nobel prize would carry. He immediately turned around.

"A lemonade, please."

"Yes, sir."

All right! Now I had some power. I felt like a kid who finds a magic wand and starts trying it out.

A few seconds went by and no lemonade; they were drinking beer, but I didn't want to drink because if I did I'd get bombed and probably end up slapping Gabo on the ass and making moves on his wife.

Hours later the lemonade came. I felt like saying to the waiter, "Excuse me? Don't you see who I'm sitting with? Jerk."

Then the question-mark man monopolized Gabo's attention; they talked about contacts and more contacts, something about Girón Beach, something about the vice-consul of Tanzania, about the interview you have for China, and are we going to Cuernavaca this weekend. I felt like a servant listening in on the talk of the rich.

I looked over at García Márquez's wife. I remembered I had read her name somewhere but I forgot what it was. Gabo stopped listening to the fat man when I asked her: "What's your name?"

"Mercedes."

"Of course," I said.

"Just like Pavlov's dog," García Márquez said, meaning me.

I didn't know what to say. My mind was racing a thousand miles a minute.

That was it, I had associated "For Mercedes. Of course", which is the dedication in Gabo's book, *Love in the Time of Cholera*. When she said, "Mercedes," I automatically thought: Of course. (I didn't really even think it, I just said it automatically; that's why it was like Pavlov's dog.)

A paranoid thought made my hands start sweating; maybe García Márquez said that because he thought I was playing some trick just to seem interesting.

It was all up to him; in the eyes of the world I would either be intelligent or an imbecile. The possibility of winning the lottery was hanging in a frightful balance. That's why I decided to say nothing and let him talk to the fat man, as if I were a child watching his father speak about strange business affairs.

Damn! Things were getting rough. I considered the possibility of going to the bathroom to take a few tokes but I knew they would be able to smell it. Besides, the second act had already started.

I did anything I could not to have to go back in. Like hell I would! I'd take the lottery any day. Besides, the best play in town was right in front of me.

Drinking my lemonade, I said to Gabo: "Hey, do you think they should legalize pot?"

"It already is," he said.

"What do you mean?"

"Well, it's as if it were."

Up comes another Ever-Present Journalist. "Señor García Márquez, I would like to do an interview with you for television."

"No," Gabo said, smiling. Good for you, Gabo! I thought.

"It will only take a moment," the lady insisted.

"No. I spend all my time writing junk for the newspapers and they still want more. Anyway, they only do it so they can say they've interviewed García Márquez." That's right, Gabo! I thought. You tell 'em! Now you have to get serious, send her to hell, although, of course, if you want I could allow her an interview with me. Har, har. Sorry, Marxists, when I get nervous I tend to be a bit of a jerk.

The lady left and then, taking over the whole table with my voice as if to say, now it's time to listen to me, quiet everyone, I said:

"Look, Gabriel. You're a very busy man. I wrote the *A Hundred Years of Solitude* of the eighties, I'm going to put in a preface and sign your name, then you'll have to sue me and it'll be a waste of your time."

Although I said it as a joke I think everyone laughed, thinking, "He'll probably do it, the smartass."

And I continued: "Anyway, I came over to you because you're García

Márquez. The truth is I'm not interested in the preface but what I really want is to win the lottery." I turned toward Mercedes. "Did you see the gringo movie about a millionaire who looks at random through the telephone book for someone to give away his money to? Well, I want to be the anonymous guy in the telephone book and I want to win me the lottery." I went on. "I have a poet friend, his name is Vicente Quirarte and he told me that as a poet he would never be as famous as José José. I want to prove him wrong."

Just then a song by José José came on the radio. The coincidence shocked me.

García Márquez turned to talk to the fat man. I felt like a fly buzzing around in the middle of Macondo. I turned back to Mercedes.

"Hey," I said to her. "I have an existential dilemma; you're going to leave soon so he can dedicate the plaque and he still hasn't said a word about my book."

"Write down your telephone number and I'll call you."

"When? In a week or in two years?"

"Next week."

García Márquez turned around and Mercedes said, "I've got myself a little son."

I made a face like a hypocritical kid asking Santa Claus for his presents. I was getting closer to the prize. You're going to pay me for this, you intellectuals! I spit on you all. Har, har, I want a lot of women. I felt like saying: "Hey, Gabo, call some girls and tell them you have a buddy who's a super-poet. No shit!"

Since I'm such a leech I started feeling really cocky. "It must be just like being Paul Newman for you," I said.

"Why?"

"Because whenever he goes to take a piss in a public bathroom the guys next to him turn around, dick and all, and as they're pissing they ask him innocently: 'Excuse me, aren't you Paul Newman?'"

He laughed. No shit! I'm so funny sometimes. Go ahead, bring the women, the photographers. Come on, you bastards!

Then we talked about some other unimportant things: for example, I asked him, "Does it bother you to be famous?"

He said yes. Smiling and with his face puckered up like that, I noticed he looked like Tin-tan, the comic.

"You can't fool me," I said. "Women make life impossible; you should have done what Lacan says: invent your own imaginary phallus."

He turned around to look at the fat man.

Then Yuppie 1 tapped García Márquez on the back and asked him to sign something so she could have his autograph.

Yuppie 2 gave him a menu so he could print his name on it with a thick pen.

Since by now we were friends I said to him: "Tell them you wrote this menu."

I wanted to seem funny. Damn right! I was adding probabilities and luck to the draw.

I had the opportunity of creating my own luck, or at least fifty per cent of it; the other fifty per cent was in the frontal lobe of the Nobel, it depended on his Gestalt or maybe on my histrionic capabilities, on my *arriviste* guilt, on the strong pull of a superego (my father) who had died three months ago, on a woman lost in the jungle of words, on a broken mirror that I used to cut myself, and to make things worse, all this without a woman, with no woman waiting to soothe my body and stretch me out like a pig in some luscious orgiastic mud.

Gabo finished writing on the menu; he couldn't refuse them. I don't know what he wrote.

We spoke a little about psychoanalysis: of how they kick psychoanalysts out of the International Psychoanalytical Association after three divorces, about how they're so holier than thou, how they're just a cheap edition of mental health, and how I was in psychoanalysis.

That was why when García Márquez came back from the bathroom I asked him: "Everything come out okay?"

"Of course," he said. I don't know if he was joking or not. "I was psychoanalyzed, too."

He sat down. "And what is your novel called?"

"*Doggie Style.*"

"Ah. And what's it about?"

"It's about a guy stuck in traffic; he wants to be a writer, to be famous, and Mike, one of the characters, tells him he should write the *A Hundred Years of Solitude* of the eighties. The guy feels happy at first but then in the middle of the traffic and the smog he realizes that there aren't any Amarantas and Aurelianos Buendías there, there aren't any José Arcadios, that all there are are drunks, gangs, poor people trampled by the yuppies—that after all, the jungle is gone."

García Márquez turned to look at the fat man.

The fat man looked at him with fervor.

For a minute I was afraid they believed I was trying to do a knock-off version of *A Hundred Years of Solitude.* But I calmed myself down and shook off my self-consciousness from my body, from my thoughts, from my sphincter. I preferred to be like Fernando Pessoa: "Only when the mind wanders can we truly let ourselves feel." I let my mind wander, looking at the ice in the lemonade. They asked for the check. García Márquez left a lot of potatoes on his plate; I was hungry and even though I felt like taking one, I didn't, I didn't want some idiot to think I was indulging a fetish or something. That's why I preferred to let my mind wander off my hunger and to watch the vice-consul and García Márquez fight over the check. We got up from the table and went through a hall until we arrived backstage. Someone announced the Nobel as "the Cervantes of our times"; they gave him his little plaque and he raised it over his head like when Rocky won the championship.

Then the group split up and someone gave me the address of the party they were having. García Márquez was carrying my book and I hoped that when he said his few words he would include: "The greatest honor of attending this event is having met Fernando Nachón; by only looking at a few pages of his book, *Doll, Do Me a Favor and Take Off Your Bra*, I am sure that Mexico has an immortal writer." But he didn't say it. I was hoping for it and at the same time I was thinking of a phrase by Elías Nandino:

"Don't write so people will call you a poet, but to fulfill yourself and avoid suicide."

I wanted to avoid suicide at all costs! Writing, shoving my name into everyone's face, whatever it took not to end up on the tracks of the subway.

I'm sorry, folks.

I climbed into the car and spotted the existence of the delicious stub of a joint; it was waiting for me like a naked woman waits for her husband when he comes home from work.

I took it in my hands and brought my lighter up to it; I singed my moustache and it smelled like burnt chicken. But I didn't care, because the smoke was tickling my bronchial tubes. It was some pot that I had gotten from Rafa, the drummer of the group Yerba Mala, 'Bad Weed', from St. Pot, Negrasska, Ollinois, Free State of America. Just two steps from the mummies of Chapultepec.

Going at seventy miles an hour on the highway I thought: I'm one step away from the Nobel Prize! Calm down! Calm down!

A police car was in front of me, going sixty. I slowed down as the blue and red lights hit me in the face. I got a craving for a Pepsi. "Just like

Pavlov's dog," I thought.

I put the roach down and took out a whole joint. I finally made it to the party.

It was great. Of course, when we got there Gurrola was already drunk and dancing cumbias, throwing his fat around in a private Dionysian dream.

"Move it, fatty!" I shouted at that black toad. But since he was totally smashed he didn't even hear me; he was dancing with a dark-skinned girl with some luscious pouty lips. I immediately went over to get a coke. Then I danced with a light-haired girl with big tits.

During a break I realized García Márquez was also there. He was standing up, looking at some paintings in the midst of the cumbias. I didn't go up to him; I didn't want to harass him, and I think no one else went up to him for the same reason.

"Poor thing," I thought. "To be the Nobel Prize must be like having an incurable disease. It's like being a leper."

And there he was: the president of Macondo, without anyone to write to him, condemned to a hundred years of solitude.

"Jesus fucking Christ!" I thought.

At the edge of the patio there was a reception 'vomitee' where about fifteen guys and girls who worked in the theater were standing around. Every time someone passed by, they contorted themselves in a bow that made them look like they were vomiting.

Then Raúl Falcó, also smashed, threw my book *Doll, Do Me a Favor and Take Off Your Bra* over to where they were standing, so when they bowed it would look like they were vomiting on it.

One of the big-assed girls from the play stopped in front of the book. They called García Márquez over.

Another girl they call Leporello screamed, drunk:

"GABOOO! GABOOOOO!"

Gabo came over and they asked him to step on the book. "No! I couldn't!" he said. "It would be better to burn it!"

It made me want to slap him upside the head and tell him: "Don't be a clown. Remember, you owe me a preface." After all, poor guy, he's sick. Those goddamn Swedes fucked him up.

He walked over my book without stepping on it and went out onto the street; my godmother Mercedes followed him and I thought: I'm not a Nobel Prize and I don't have Mercedes. Shit shit shit!

I returned to the party.

Mongo told me, "If he does the preface for you then everyone who's screwed you over will say: 'Goddamn! Then we were the idiots after all.'"

"I don't think so," I told him. "Not everyone likes García Márquez."

"So what do you think of him?"

"I don't really know," I said. "He has a look that Onetti might call 'sickly, almost affected.' But then I'm trying to think for Onetti."

"Affected?" Mongo asked me.

"Oh fuck it. Why do I bother talking about these things with you? Now you're going to run off to the Nueve to tell everyone. Sure! Soon they'll all be saying that García Márquez is a swish. Stop joking around, asshole."

Mongo, laughing, said, "Jeeeeeesus you'll see, I'm going to say that you said that García Márquez is a faggot. Jeeeesus. Now you fucked up."

Since I knew he was half drunk I laughed at his bullshit. We went out to take a hit and I told him I would write about this without even knowing if García Márquez was going to write the preface or not.

That's why I wrote it beforehand. So I wouldn't come out for him or against him. Besides, I know he's very sick and I don't want to hurt him. There's enough cruelty towards a Nobel prizewinner without some fly in the middle of Macondo buzzing in his face.

I go back to the party to watch Tiresias (Gurrola) jiggling the lard as he sweats alcohol in front of a dark-skinned girl with lips that are puckered and ready to go.

"Move it, fatty," I shouted enviously.

P.S.
If a preface by García Márquez shows up in this book then yes, I did win the lottery. I'll be rich and, betraying Borges, fall headlong into the most vulgar banality of all. Sniff. Sorry, Marxists. When I think about fame I get really nervous.

P.P.S.
Mercedes still hasn't called me ....

www.ingramcontent.com/pod-product-compliance
Ingram Content Group UK Ltd.
Pitfield, Milton Keynes, MK11 3LW, UK
UKHW021053270726
13967UKWH00012B/636

9 781425 158316